It's hard not to give up when everything seems hopeless . . .

"Junior may not make it," Mrs. Kingsley said.

Ashley felt as if she'd just swallowed a rock. She loved all the horses on the ranch, but Junior was special. "Oh, Mom," she wailed, "why? Why is everything going so wrong?"

"Difficult, heartbreaking things happen sometimes," her mother said.

"But I used to feel like no matter what happened, someone would help me; I was never all alone. I even believed I had an angel watching over me." Ashley laughed bitterly. "An angel. Can you believe it?"

"Angels are a nice idea. I wish they *were* real," her mother said. "You're not alone, though. You always have Dad and me."

"I heard you and Dad talking," Ashley said slowly. "Mom, are you and Dad getting divorced?"

Mrs. Kingsley turned to face her.

Ashley returned her gaze, barely daring to breathe. *Say no*, she found herself praying silently. *Say, no, we have some problems, but we're working them out. Everything will be all right.*

"It's time you knew, Ashley," said Mrs. Kingsley quietly. "Your father and I are seeing a lawyer. We're getting a divorce."

Win a Guardian Angel Pin!
See back of book for details.

Ashley's Lost Angel

FOREVER ANGELS

Ashley's Lost Angel

Suzanne Weyn

Rainbow Bridge®

Troll Associates

Text copyright © 1995 by Chardiet Unlimited, Inc., and Suzanne Weyn.
Cover illustration copyright © 1995 by Mark English.
Cover border photography by Katrina.
Angel stickers (GS11) copyright © by Gallery Graphics, Inc., Noel, MO, 64854. Used with permission.

Published by Troll Associates, Inc. Rainbow Bridge is a trademark of Troll Associates.

Printed in the United States of America.

10 9 8 7 6 5 4 3 2 1

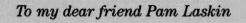

To my dear friend Pam Laskin

1

"Come on, Junior, come on," Ashley urged in a desperate whisper. "You've got to try. Fight it, Junior. Don't let it beat you like this!"

The palomino colt lying in the straw beside her lifted his head and looked up with dull, glazed eyes. Ashley knelt over him, stroking his cream-colored mane. For a brief moment, Ashley saw a flicker of the lively spark that used to shine in Junior's dark eyes. But in the next second it died out like a flame in the wind.

She stood and brushed straw from her jeans. Feeling completely helpless, she gazed around the stable. Ropes, saddles, blankets, shovels, brushes, and pails hung from the walls or nestled in corners. The moist smell of horses and hay filled the air. She listened to the muffled sound of the horses moving in their stalls, heard their snorts and whinnies.

"Why isn't he better, Alice, why?" Ashley asked the tall blonde woman in the next stall. Alice was the ranch hand. She had been working on Ashley's parents' horse farm for years. She didn't really expect Alice to know. She just wished there was someone to ask who *would* know. Dr. Jeffers, the vet, obviously didn't have the answer—otherwise Junior would be getting better.

"The antibiotic might take a while to kick in," Alice said, as she brushed down Junior's mother, May. "Dr. Jeffers told us that, remember?"

"I know," Ashley recalled glumly. But how long was "a while"? Junior had been sick for four days now, and nothing they did seemed to help. If anything, he seemed worse.

Ashley leaned back against the door to Junior's stall and fretfully ran her hand through her strawberry-blonde curls.

May stretched her brown-and-cream spotted head over into Junior's stall. She whinnied gently at her child, who would be a year old in June. Junior lifted his nose to her, snorting softly.

Ashley watched the silent communication between mother and child. Something very like human love flowed between them. Ashley had been born there on the ranch, and in her whole life of being around horses she'd never seen a mother and colt who were so close.

"Poor Junior," Ashley said soothingly. She couldn't stand seeing him so miserable. Junior had always been an odd horse, in a nice sort of way. He was more affectionate than the other colts and fillies that had been born at the ranch the previous spring. When he saw Ashley, he always trotted over to greet her. Right from the start, he'd made it clear that he knew her and liked her.

But as spring had turned to summer and fall, then to

winter, Junior didn't seem to mature in the same way the other young horses did. He was smaller than the other colts, and quieter. He didn't join them in their wild chases around the pasture. Instead, he hung back and stayed with May. Most colts and fillies were independent of their mothers by now. But Junior, who looked almost exactly like his cream-and-brown-spotted palomino dam, wouldn't be separated from her.

Ashley understood how he felt. She couldn't imagine ever being far from her own mother, even after she was grown up. As the only females in their family, Ashley and her mother had a special bond. Her mother was the one she could always talk to, the one she counted on for advice. When Ashley envisioned her future, she saw herself working on the horse ranch, helping her parents run it, especially as they got older. It was a good feeling to think that, even then, she'd have her mother close by.

Ashley could see her future clearly. She easily imagined herself coming into the house after a day of leading trail rides. Maybe she'd be married, and her husband would work on the ranch, too. They'd have some kids. She pictured her strawberry-blonde mother—gray-haired by then—in the house baking cookies with her grandchildren—Ashley's children. She'd smile at Ashley as she walked into the kitchen and say she was doing a fine job with the ranch. Ashley imagined herself smiling back, happy to have her own children in her mother's warm care.

May's sad whinny broke into Ashley's daydream. Ashley looked down at Junior, lying there so weak, and wondered again what could be wrong with him. Dr. Jeffers hadn't been sure, but she'd said it was probably some sort of infection. She'd prescribed a bottle of very large brown pills and said she'd return at the end of the following week to check up on Junior.

To Ashley, the week seemed to be taking forever.

A slab of sunlight suddenly cut across the shadowy stable. Ashley turned and saw Christina standing in the doorway. Her long, corn-colored hair shone, illuminated by the sunlight at her back. "How's the patient?" she asked, as she came in. She leaned forward to hang on the chest-high door.

"Not good," Ashley told her.

"Too bad," Christina sympathized. The small white scar across her left eyebrow—the reminder of a childhood spill off a pony—crinkled slightly as she frowned. "Poor little guy," she said. Her sky-blue eyes filled with concern as she looked down at Junior.

"Christina, did you finish cleaning your room?" Alice inquired, putting the final brushstrokes to May.

"Not exactly, Mom," Christina admitted sheepishly. "But I was doing something extremely important. Two things, really. But I *swear* I'll do my room before dinner tonight. Honest."

"What was so important?" Alice asked.

Christina's face brightened with enthusiasm. "I didn't get a chance to tell either of you, because it just happened this morning." She paused dramatically, her sky-blue eyes darting between Ashley and her mother as if she were checking to be sure they could withstand the sheer excitement of what she was about to tell them. "I might have my very own column in the *Writer*," she declared, referring to the Pine Ridge Middle School newspaper.

"Cool! What kind of column?" Ashley asked. "And how did you hear about it on a Saturday morning?"

"Katie just called me," Christina replied excitedly. "It's a horoscope column."

Ashley's green eyes went wide with disbelief. "*Katie* offered you a *horoscope* column?" she laughed incredulously. "Katie, who doesn't believe in any of that stuff? Are you kidding?"

"Well, yeah. You know, Katie just started writing and taking pictures for the *Writer* at the end of April. She was talking to Sally Overton, the editor, yesterday afternoon, and Sally told her she wanted to add a horoscope column, so Katie suggested me for the job. She told Sally she'd ask me if I wanted to do it."

"Oh. So it was really Sally's idea, not Katie's, right?" Ashley demanded.

"Well, yes, whatever," Christina waved one hand vaguely.

That made sense. Ashley would have been totally shocked if their friend Katie had suggested the column. Katie was the original skeptic. She didn't believe anything unless she'd seen it—and even then she was cautious. "Like that old saying goes," Katie often said, "believe half of what you see—and none of what you hear."

Ashley remembered the first day Katie had arrived at school—that past March. She'd glared at everyone with angry eyes from beneath the brim of her baseball cap. A real tough kid, everyone thought. But Ashley had noticed that despite her intimidating glare, Katie never directly met anyone's eyes. Instead, she fiddled with a pack of cigarettes, pulling at the cellophane, packing it against her palm, sometimes even taking out a cigarette and rolling it between her fingers.

Ashley had also noticed that the pack of cigarettes never emptied—or changed. It was always the same pack, only growing more dirty and frayed over time. She'd never seen Katie smoke a single cigarette, either. Ashley had finally realized the cigarettes were just a prop, a way for Katie to appear tough. From that moment, Ashley had understood how anxious and frightened Katie really was about being in a new school.

It wasn't only the unused cigarettes that had made Ashley interested in Katie. Something in Katie's hazel eyes had told Ashley there was someone worth knowing behind her bad-girl routine.

She'd been right, too. Katie had turned out to be a good friend, much more warm and approachable than anyone would have thought. Katie had just had an awful time. Ashley shuddered to think *how* awful. Ashley couldn't imagine losing your parents and having to move from the only home you'd ever known.

In the past few weeks, Katie had become a close friend of Ashley and Christina. And the almost unbelievable things they'd been through together had cemented their friendship. Even so, Katie could still barely tolerate all Christina's new-age, spiritual, other-worldly interests. *That* hadn't changed.

Christina opened the stall door and stepped in. She took a quick look over at her mother and then lowered her head. "You know, Ashley," Christina murmured, "I don't think Katie's as disbelieving as you think. Don't you think she's changed a little since . . . you know, since we saw the. . ."

"You mean the angels?" Ashley whispered.

Christina nodded, again glancing surreptitiously at her mother.

Ashley still couldn't understand how Christina's mother could disbelieve their story about seeing the angels. Alice had been a flower child in the Woodstock era. Like her daughter, she believed in all kinds of new age stuff that a lot of other people—*most* other people—would call bunk. Different-colored crystals adorned the windows and shelves of their cabin. A pack of tarot cards sat on the mantel, along with many books on astrology, herbal medicine, healing massage, numerology, and other offbeat subjects.

Yet when Christina had told Alice that Katie, Ashley, and Christina had had a real-life experience with angels, had actually seen and spoken to three real angels, open-minded Alice—of all people—had refused to believe it.

"Maybe you *felt* some sort of spiritual presence," she'd suggested, grudgingly.

"No, Mom, they were completely real!" Christina had insisted. Ashley had been with her and had seen the worried look on Alice's face. Alice couldn't accept it, no matter how open she was to other mysterious, supernatural goings-on. "Maybe I've filled your head with too many spiritual ideas," Alice worried aloud. "Perhaps you're not ready for them yet, and they've confused you."

"I'm not telling Mom any more about the angels," Christina later told Ashley. "I think she's considering sending me to a psychiatrist because of it."

Because she'd witnessed Alice's reaction, Ashley decided against confiding in her own parents. Her experience with the angels was the only thing Ashley had ever held back from telling them.

She didn't want to hear their disbelief. She cherished her encounter with the angels. It was the most amazing thing that had ever happened to her. She didn't want any doubt shed on it, especially not by people as important to her as her parents.

But no matter how carefully Ashley guarded the experience by keeping it to herself, time was tarnishing her absolute faith in what she'd seen. It was just so . . . *unbelievable.*

The more time passed, the more Ashley began to doubt what she'd seen. Her own logical mind was telling her the very same things she feared her parents might say.

No one ever really *saw* angels.

It was all a nice story, but not truly real.

She must have *wanted* to believe those people were angels, and her imagination had simply taken over.

But while Ashley listened to the logical part of her mind, another part cried out inside her, saying, *It was real! You know what you saw. It was real.* This inner battle left Ashley feeling completely confused. She just didn't know what to think anymore about the angels.

"Ashley, I mean, don't *you* think Katie isn't as doubting about mystical, unexplainable kinds of things now?" Christina went on in a whisper.

"A *little* less, maybe," Ashley allowed. Even though Katie had seen the angels, she, too, had begun to doubt her own eyes. And she certainly didn't accept anything else—like horoscopes or tarot cards—that she couldn't explain logically.

At that moment one of Ashley's seventeen-year-old twin brothers, Jeremy, stuck his head in the stable. His red curls, which he wore short at the sides and longish at the back, and his bright green eyes made him look like an older, male version of Ashley. "Oh, Ashley, your boyyy-friennnd just called," he sang out teasingly.

Ashley jumped to her feet. "Trevor?" she asked eagerly, ignoring the mockery in Jeremy's voice.

"I guess so, whatever," Jeremy answered in a bored voice. "He didn't want to wait for me to come out and get you. He said for you to call him back."

Ashley brushed more straw from her neatly pressed jeans and raked her hair with one hand as if Trevor might suddenly materialize out of nowhere. "I'd better call him back right away," she told Christina.

"What's happening with the two of you?" Christina asked, petting Junior.

"I'm pretty sure he likes me. He asked me to go to the movies with him at the mall tonight," Ashley said happily as she headed out of the stall.

She couldn't help feeling happy when she thought about tonight. They would be with a group of other kids, Trevor's friends. So it wasn't a *real* date. Ashley was glad of that, since her mom and dad had said she couldn't date until she was fourteen. Still, Trevor *had* asked her out.

"Go call him back," Christina prompted, following.

Ashley nodded. "Okay. I'll call him right now," she said, "Wait, okay?" She took off, running toward the house.

2

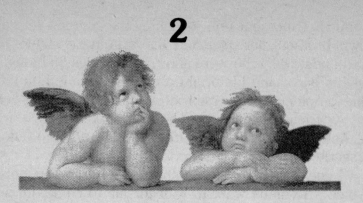

On her way, Ashley crossed the wide dirt path that separated their low rambling, ranch-style house from the stable. She waved to her father, who was leading a group of riders returning from a trail ride out of the Pine Manor Woods, just beyond the stable. Her father waved back, but he didn't smile as he usually did when he saw his only daughter.

Ashley looked at his serious, weathered face and realized he hadn't smiled much at all in the last two weeks. She made a mental note to ask him if he was feeling all right. But right now, she couldn't stop. She had to call Trevor back. Nothing was more important than that.

Bounding up onto the porch of her house, Ashley leapt over Champ, the family's golden retriever. He looked up, probably expecting her to ruffle the top of his head, as usual, but right now she was in too much of a hurry.

"Mom!" she called as she entered the sunny house.

"In here," her mother called from the den, just off the living room. The den functioned as the front office for the Pine Manor Ranch, which the Kingsley family had run for three generations. Her petite, red-headed mother sat hunched over a large accounts ledger, her delicate brows knit into a scowl of unhappy concentration. Her pinched face softened into a smile when she looked up at Ashley. "Hi, sweetie. What is it?"

"Could I use the phone in your room?"

"Why not use the kitchen phone?"

"I'd like some privacy."

"Use the kitchen phone," her mother insisted mildly as she turned back to her ledger. "There's no one in the kitchen."

Ashley sighed as she headed for the kitchen. She wished her parents would let her have her own phone, in her room. A lot of other girls in the eighth grade did. But Ashley's parents couldn't understand why anyone needed *so* much privacy.

In the kitchen, Ashley punched in Trevor's number. Even though she'd only called him once before, she knew the number by heart. She'd memorized everything about Trevor, his big brown eyes, the way his blond bangs brushed his eyebrows, his adorable sideways smile.

After four rings, Trevor picked up the phone. "Hello?"

"Hi, it's Ashley. You wanted me to call you back."

"Oh, yeah. Ashley. Hi. Listen, something came up. I mean, I don't feel real well and I don't think I can make it to the movies tonight. I won't be able to, I mean." He held the phone away from his mouth and coughed a dry, raspy cough to demonstrate his sickness.

A stab of disappointment ran through Ashley. Unexpectedly, a lump formed in her throat, but she fought it down. The last thing she wanted was to sound like a pouty brat over the phone. "That's too bad," she said as evenly as she could manage. "Have you been to the doctor?"

"Ah, yeah," Trevor replied. "He said to take it easy."

"Did he say what was the matter with you?"

"You know, a flu kind of thing."

"Well, I hope you feel better."

"Thanks. I guess I'll see you in school Monday."

"But won't you be too sick?" Ashley asked.

"Oh, well, I'll just have to see how it goes. Maybe I'll see you, maybe I won't."

"All right. Well, bye. I hope you feel better," Ashley said as she hung up.

She leaned against the wall of her cheerful yellow kitchen. Was it possible Trevor wasn't telling her the truth? she wondered. He'd sounded more nervous than sick. Maybe he'd changed his mind about her. What if he wasn't interested in her, after all? But he'd seemed so interested the last few days. Hadn't he even carried her tray for her at lunchtime yesterday? Why would he suddenly change his mind?

Ashley's shoulders slumped miserably.

Maybe he really was sick. Maybe she was just being a big baby about this. It was just that she was already upset about Junior, and she'd hoped going to the movies with Trevor would cheer her up. She was sure it would have.

Well, she thought, pushing herself off of the wall, there was nothing she could do about it, anyway. She stood a moment and studied her reflection in the kitchen window. Cocking her head to the side, she turned so that her face was reflected in the window at a three-quarter angle. Then she tossed her long curls over her shoulder. Yes, she decided, that was her most attractive side. Definitely.

In her heart, she knew she was a pretty girl. All her life, people had said so. How could she *not* know it?

All right, maybe she wished she were taller, like Katie or Christina. She didn't *adore* being petite like her mother. Still, it wasn't the worst thing in the world. And she knew she always presented herself well. She took time with her clothes and grooming and even wore just a little makeup sometimes. She carefully pressed her jeans and shirts. She always made sure her nail polish was perfect. She kept her wild red hair tamed to gently frame her face.

On the whole, Ashley was pleased with the image reflected back at her in the window. Why shouldn't Trevor like her? He was probably just *really* sick.

Still disappointed but feeling a little less insecure, Ashley headed toward the living room. Her father had come in from his ride and stood in the den talking to her mother, his broad-shouldered back toward Ashley.

"Would you calm down, Judy," he spoke to Mrs. Kingsley in a tense voice. "You're making this into a bigger deal than it is."

"How can you say that, Hank!" Mrs. Kingsley exclaimed. "You don't handle the accounts. I do. I know what I'm talking about. We are in big trouble."

Big trouble? Ashley froze. What kind of big trouble?

She quietly backed up toward the kitchen doorway so they wouldn't see her eavesdropping.

"Come on, Judy," Mr. Kingsley said lightly. "Don't exaggerate."

"That attitude infuriates me!" Mrs. Kingsley yelled at him. "You ride around and play with the horses all day, and you pay no attention to the real work of running this ranch."

Ashley held herself tightly. She seldom heard her parents fight. And she'd never heard them speak this angrily to one another. To hear them yell like this was a new—and frightening—experience.

"Play with the horses!" Mr. Kingsley cried angrily. "Is that what you think I do all day? Play with the horses?"

"Whatever you're doing, it's not bringing in enough money to keep this ranch going!" Mrs. Kingsley shot back.

"You're the one who is supposed to be in charge of the money," Mr. Kingsley accused her.

"I can't manage money when there is no money there to manage," Mrs. Kingsley defended herself.

Ashley couldn't see her mother clearly, but from her voice, she could tell she had begun to cry.

"Hank, lately I don't feel like we're in this together anymore," Mrs. Kingsley spoke through her tears. "I've been worried about money for months, and when I try to talk to you about it, you just tell me not to worry. It's like you don't even listen."

"I listen," Mr. Kingsley insisted coldly. "I've been worried and thinking about how we might get more horses to board here, which would bring in cash each month. Don't accuse me of not listening. I just deal with things differently than you do."

"You deal with things by thinking about them for ten minutes and then forgetting about them!" Mrs. Kingsley's voice rose again. "If you've been thinking about getting horses to board, why haven't you gone out and gotten some boarders? Thinking isn't going to save us if you don't *do* something!"

"When do you think I should do more than I'm already doing, Judy? I do a full day's work as it is!"

"So do I! We have a mountain of debt, Hank. But you keep riding around *thinking* about what we should do!"

"That isn't fair, Judy. You don't know what it's like to put in the kind of day I do each day."

"Oh, I can't talk to you anymore!" Mrs. Kingsley wailed. "I don't know how much more of it I can take. I'm serious, Hank. I really am! This ranch is going under, and so is our marriage!"

Mrs. Kingsley stormed from the den and slammed out the front door. Mr. Kingsley just stood still for a moment, then he stomped angrily out of the house, too.

Ashley leaned hard against the kitchen doorway. Her mother's voice echoed in her whirling head. *This ranch is going under and so is our marriage!*

Was it really possible?

Of course it was *possible*. She always saw ads for going out of business sales. Businesses failed every day. The ranch seemed like so much more than just a business. Yet it was a business. And it *could* fail to make money.

But her parents, could their marriage fail?

No! Not her parents.

But so many kids in her class had divorced parents. It was the most possible thing in the world.

Ashley's stomach lurched and she stumbled into the kitchen. Sitting down hard on a chair, she gripped its back to keep the room from spinning.

Until this moment she'd had no idea things were bad. Not with the ranch or with her parents.

Apparently there was a lot she hadn't noticed.

3

"Did she actually use the word, *divorce*?" Christina asked later that afternoon as she and Ashley sat on the scrubby grass behind the stable.

Ahead of them, several yards away, the sweet-scented pines that gave Pine Manor Woods its name rustled softly.

Ashley shook her head. "No, she didn't say that exact word. But what else does it mean when you say your marriage is going under?"

"I suppose," Christina agreed, sighing. She stirred a patch of dirt with a long stick she'd absently picked up earlier as they walked. "I know! I'll do a tarot card reading for you later. Maybe it'll help give us some idea of how things are really going."

"Okay," Ashley agreed as she rested her head on her knees. She wasn't sure she believed in the ability of tarot cards to foretell the future. But according to Christina, the cards were just one of many methods of foretelling the future. Christina knew the tarot cards best, though now she was trying to teach herself numerology, the study of numbers, and the I Ching, an ancient Chinese form of fortune telling.

Ashley couldn't fully believe in any of it.

But she didn't *not* believe it, either.

After all, it *might* be true. Lots of people believed in those things. Katie always insisted that none of it could be true because it didn't make sense. You couldn't explain how it worked in any reasonable way.

Maybe, though, Ashley thought, it just worked in ways people didn't understand.

And then there was Christina, herself. She did seem to have an ability to *know* things she couldn't possibly know. She had strong feelings about things, feelings that were often right.

It had occurred to Ashley that Christina might use stuff like the tarot cards just as a way to focus her mind on a problem and let her hunches, intuitions and feelings come through. Even if Ashley didn't believe in any other part of it, she had faith in Christina's hunches.

Christina had come to the ranch with her mother five years before, when both girls were just eight. Ashley was thrilled. With two older brothers in the house, she was glad to have a girl her own age living in a cabin right on the ranch.

Living out here on the ranch had meant that Ashley was separated from the other kids, who lived near one another, closer to the town of Pine Ridge. Until Christina arrived, Ashley had often felt lonely.

That all changed, though. Having Christina there meant Ashley always had someone to play with.

Through the years they'd grown very close. Now they were like the best kind of sisters—not necessarily alike, but accepting of one another's differences.

"Divorce isn't the end of the world, you know," Christina pointed out thoughtfully.

"It would be the end of *my* world," Ashley grumbled.

Christina's father had left them when Christina was just a baby. She didn't know what it was like to live with both parents. It had always been just Christina and her mother. But Ashley *did* know what it was like to live with both parents, and the thought of living with only one of them at a time was unbearable to her.

How could she ever chose between her mother and her father?

What if a judge sent the boys with her dad and she stayed with her mother? That would be horrible! As big pains as Jeremy and Jason could be sometimes, Ashley couldn't imagine life without them. No, she couldn't even think about any of it. It made her head hurt.

"This is a problem for me, too, you know," Christina said.

"Thanks. I know you always care about my problems," Ashley said.

"Sure I do, but that's not exactly what I meant. If the ranch folds or is sold, my mom and I might have to move, too."

Ashley hadn't even thought of that! "I guess so," she agreed unhappily. Not only was her family about to break up, but she would also lose her best friend—a best friend who was practically a sister to her. Everything just kept looking worse and worse.

At that moment, a tall, slim girl with straight, should-length brown hair came around the corner of the stable. "Hi, guys," she said as she took a seat beside them on the sparse grass. "Alice told me you were back here."

"Hi," the girls greeted Katie with one voice.

Katie looked quickly from Christina to Ashley and her wide, expressive mouth twisted to one side. "What?" she asked after a moment. "Something's the matter. What's wrong?"

Ashley laughed bitterly. "Gee, I don't know where to start."

"Start anywhere," Katie suggested seriously.

"The ranch is going out of business, my parents might be getting divorced, Junior is still sick, and I was supposed to go to the movies with Trevor tonight but now I'm not because he says he's sick, but I'm not sure I believe him," Ashley rapidly ticked off her woes.

"Oh, is that all?" Katie said drily.

Ashley rolled her eyes miserably.

Suddenly, Christina got to her knees. The color of her sky-blue eyes deepened with excitement. "I know what to do!" she cried.

"About what?" Ashley asked.

"About all of it," Christina replied. "I know how we can solve all your problems, Ashley!"

"Uh-oh," Katie moaned, slumping back against the stable wall. "*Please* don't tell her to stand on her head and chant so she can absorb positive energies from the earth or anything weird like that."

"That's not a bad idea," said Christina, too excited by her own thoughts to be put off by Katie's sarcasm. "But it wasn't what I was thinking."

"What were you thinking?" Ashley asked.

"The angels," Christina spoke with a quiet intensity. "We'll find the angels and ask them for help."

"Now *there's* an idea," Katie said, her voice rich with irony. "I'll just go get the phone book and look up *Angels*. I'm sure they're listed."

"Very funny." Christina grimaced, unamused. "Of course they're not in the phone book. But we can go into the woods and find them."

"I am *not* doing another one of those chanting circles with those crystal things and the statue and all," Katie insisted firmly. "The last time you made us do that, I felt like a total jerk. And besides, it didn't even work."

Ashley smiled gently at the memory. Christina had once set up a stone circle in the woods for the specific purpose of calling the angels to them. She'd made Ashley and Katie twirl and chant around a statue of an angel and some amethyst crystals she'd claimed would bring greater energy into their circle. Their experiment had met with no response whatsoever.

"No, Katie, we're not going to do that again," Christina said impatiently. "We're going to go look for the bridge."

"The Angels Crossing Bridge?" asked Katie.

"Why not?" Christina responded. "That's were you met them the first time. I bet they live there. Or it's a power spot where they can cross over between worlds."

"You and your power spots. I still don't get it," Katie said, scornfully.

"I've explained it to you a million times," said Christina.

"Hardly a million," Katie said. "Explain it again, why don't you?"

Christina rolled her eyes and spoke in a slow voice as if she were talking to a child. "A power spot is a place where positive energy collects, like a pool of water—only it's not water, it's energy. It's a very good place, and spirits from the other world find it easy to pass back and forth at power spots. My mother thinks the woods are full of them."

"No wonder I can't understand it," said Katie, pulling the brim of her baseball cap around to the back. "It makes no sense."

"It doesn't have to make sense," Christina insisted.

Katie groaned and pressed her palms to her face in a gesture of total frustration.

"But we're not sure where the bridge is," Ashley reminded Christina. "And remember how lost we got the last time we went deep into the woods."

"All right. Suit yourselves," said Christina with a disappointed but resigned air. "Sit back and do nothing if you like."

Ashley stared into the piny woods. Its rustling needles seemed to whisper, to call to her.

What if Christina were right, she thought. If they really had seen angels, maybe they could help. "It might be worth a try," Ashley said, speaking to herself as much as to her friends. "We still have hours of daylight. Now that it's spring, it's staying light later and later."

"Oh, come on," Katie objected. "It's crazy to go looking for angels."

"How can you say that?" Christina gasped, "After

everything that happened! After what we *saw!*"

"I'm not so sure we saw it," Katie said.

"What?" Christina yelped.

"I know we thought we saw angels, but maybe we just saw three people dressed in white outside the hospital that night. After all, doctors and nurses do wear white. And it was snowing. The light from the hospital might have made them seem like they were glowing. The three of us were really tired. Who knows what we really saw?"

"I know," Christina said confidently. "We saw angels."

They looked to Ashley for her opinion.

"I don't know," she admitted with a shrug. "I just don't know anymore."

"What about those people—Edwina, Norma, and Ned—the ones who saved us that time in the woods?" Christina insisted. "They practically admitted they were angels. Katie, they changed your life!"

"They were just three nice and extremely strange people who hung out in the woods," Katie reasoned, not meeting Christina's insistent glare. "I don't know what you're talking about."

Christina stood. "Well, I'm going to look for the bridge. You two can stay here if you like."

Ashley scrambled to her feet. "I'll come with you. I wouldn't mind taking a walk."

"All right," Katie agreed grudgingly as she got up and dusted grass from the seat of her jeans. "I'll come, too."

Christina smiled at them. "Great."

At the border of the forest, the sun danced on the forest floor as it filtered down through the pine branches. It played on low-growing bushes, small sapling trees, and the first purple and yellow wild-flowers that were beginning to edge their way up at the base of trees and in the mossy cracks of the boulders scattered here and there among the trees.

A brown-and-green blanket of fallen pine needles muffled their footsteps. The only sounds were the occasional twig breaking and the light scampering noise of an unseen animal fleeing their intrusion.

In the midst of this hushed world the girls' voices rang out, seemingly amplified by the quiet surrounding them. "There are a few more things I want to tell you about the column," Katie spoke to Christina authoritatively. "I didn't tell you this on the phone because I thought I should say it in person. Since I recommended you for this column, I don't want you to embarrass me, okay? When you write the column, don't be advising kids at school to sleep with rocks under their pillows or—"

"Crystals," Christina prompted her.

"What?" Katie asked.

"I sleep with a crystal under my pillow. Not any old rock," said Christina.

"Whatever," said Katie, ignoring the distinction. "Don't tell kids to do that."

"Why shouldn't I?" Christina challenged her.

"Because they want advice like 'Beware of romantic problems this month.' Stuff like 'At the end of the month you will win a big prize.'"

"I know, but if I see trouble ahead for a particular sign of the zodiac, I want to advise my readers on how to center their energies in a meaningful way," Christina insisted.

Katie sighed loudly. "Just write, 'Look out this month. Big trouble ahead. Lay low.'"

"That's not very helpful advice," Christina sniffed.

"I knew you were going to say something like that!" Katie cried in exasperation. "You can't write about using crystals or chanting. Kids will think you're weird. They'll think *I'm* weird for being your friend. They'll think Ashley is weird, too."

"Who cares what a few closed-minded individuals might think. Is it my column or isn't it?" Christina asked pointedly.

"Why did I even suggest that you write this column?" Katie moaned. "Me and my big mouth!"

Ashley picked up her pace to put some distance between herself and her bickering friends. Often, it was Ashley who made peace between them. It seemed to be her unofficial role. But today she had no energy to play go-between. She had her own pressing problems to worry about, her own thoughts to unravel.

If they succeeded in finding the bridge, would the angels be there? How would they look this time? She knew they sometimes disguised themselves as people. But she'd also seen the three angels in all their shining, celestial glory. She couldn't get the picture of them out of her head. It was the most awesome sight she'd ever seen—the impossibly huge wings, the incredible, nearly blinding glow. Shimmering. Iridescent. No sight could have been more mesmerizing.

How could she have imagined it? What she'd seen was beyond her imagination.

She wasn't sure she was ready for such an overwhelming experience on an ordinary Saturday afternoon. Hearing that her parents might divorce had been overwhelming enough for one day.

Besides, maybe this was just a crazy idea, anyway. Even if they *had* seen the angels before, perhaps it was just one of those once-in-a-lifetime experiences.

Maybe it was dumb to think they could just call up an angel whenever they wanted. It wasn't the sort of thing the average, normal person did. If it was, people would be calling them all the time. Everyone would talk about it.

No, this really was crazy, she decided. Still, despite her certainty that they were wasting their time, some desperate hope deep within made her continue.

They had now walked far enough into the forest so the canopy of branches above blocked out all but the slimmest lines of wavering sunlight. There was less plant life on the ground. Instead, odd-shaped mushrooms occasionally broke through the pine-needle floor in small, brownish yellow clusters or formed a golden shelf on a tree trunk. The boulders were dotted only with moss and creeping, shade-loving vines.

Ashley noticed that the air was wetter here, and colder.

Behind Ashley, Katie and Christina had stopped their combative talk. They moved along carefully, watching the ground for fallen trees or rocks, each girl appearing to be caught up in her own private thoughts, as if the place had made them a part of its deep, all-encompassing silence.

Ashley wasn't entirely sure where they were headed.

Katie might know better. She was the only one who had ever been to the Angels Crossing Bridge.

"Is this the right way?" Ashley called back over her shoulder to Katie.

"I think so," Katie replied, frowning thoughtfully. "I'm not positive, though." She stopped and looked around. "There!" she cried, darting off to the left. "There's the stream I followed."

Ashley and Christina joined Katie at a narrow stream, at no place more than two yards wide. It flowed along quietly over flat rocks and sticks. "How do you know this is the same stream?" Ashley wanted to know.

"I don't, really," Katie admitted. "But I know I followed a stream that led to the creek where the Angels Crossing Bridge was. Right now, this is the only stream I see. So . . . "

"Might as well follow it," Ashley agreed.

"Let's go," Christina said gamely.

They followed the stream, leaping back and forth across it once in a while, just for fun. Ashley still had no idea whether or not they were going in the right direction.

She also realized she'd lost track of the time, which was unusual for her. Normally she had an excellent sense of how much time had passed. But now she wasn't sure if they'd been walking for a half an hour or an hour, or even longer. And she couldn't judge by looking at the sky, since the pines blocked it from view. Still, there *was* enough light to see, so it must be okay.

After a while, the stream disappeared into the ground at the base of a low hill. "Now what?" Ashley asked Katie.

"I remember climbing a hill before I found the bridge. Let's go up," Katie suggested.

Midway up the hill, Ashley became aware of a distant sound. She stopped to listen more carefully. *Water!* she realized. It was the crisp, restless sound of moving water.

"The creek!" she shouted excitedly, breaking into a run. She was the first to reach the crest of the hill. There, on the other side, just as she'd hoped, was the creek. The trees opened here, showing a wide band of blue sky. Sunlight poured down and the water reflected it back, making the rushing water sparkle with dazzling light.

"There's the bridge!" Ashley shouted.

Spanning the creek was an old, covered wooden bridge. Its roof spanned the bridge entirely on top, but it was enclosed only halfway up the sides, giving a view of anything on the bridge. Whatever road had once led to and from the bridge had long since been overgrown with pines.

"That's it, isn't it?" Ashley said to Katie, who had joined her at the top of the hill.

Katie nodded as she fixed her eyes on the bridge.

"We found it!" gasped Christina, reaching the top of the hill. "It's the Angels Crossing Bridge!"

Ashley gazed at the bridge. Picturesque as it was, she couldn't help but be flooded with disappointment. "There's no one there," she said discontentedly, turning away. She took a step back down the hill. Suddenly Christina caught hold of her arm.

"Yes, there is!" Christina cried excitedly. "Look!"

4

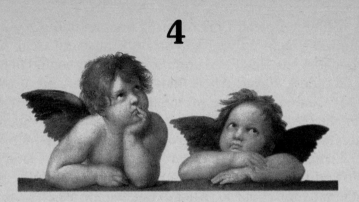

Ashley looked back sharply and saw two deer—a doe and a young buck—standing on the bridge. "Where did they come from?" she asked.

"From the other side, I guess," Christina replied.

"The other side of the bridge?" Ashley asked, in case Christina was referring to a more mystical "other side."

"I just noticed them there all of a sudden," Christina said noncommittally.

"So did I," agreed Katie. "They weren't there a second ago."

The deer stood absolutely still in the middle of the bridge. They stared expectantly up at the girls.

"Let's go down and see them," Christina suggested.

"Why?" asked Katie. "They're just deer."

Ashley stared at the deer. Something about them was unusual. She couldn't figure out what it was, though.

Christina began heading over the crest of the hill toward the bridge. "I don't know. It's just a feeling I have," she said quietly by way of explanation.

Ashley followed Christina. If Christina had a feeling, then she was willing to follow. Checking over her shoulder, she saw Katie start down the hill behind her.

The deer stayed where they were, their large brown eyes trained on the approaching girls. Every so often, the doe flicked her high, white flag of a tail as if slightly nervous about the ever-narrowing gap between them.

When they were several yards from the bridge, Christina slowed her pace. Ashley, too, walked as carefully and quietly as she could so as not to frighten the deer.

As they got closer, Ashley realized what was odd about the deer. The buck and the doe were standing calmly beside one another.

Male and female deer normally didn't travel together. Ashley had lived around deer all her life. They came to the edge of the woods, especially in winter, when food was scarce. She'd seen a lone buck, or, in spring, a doe with fawns, even several does together, or bucks in a group. But she'd never seen a buck and a doe travel together. From what she knew of deer, they just didn't do that.

Maybe there *was* something unusual about these two.

Christina was the first to reach the entrance to the bridge. By now, the deer should have bolted, Ashley realized. But they hadn't. She'd never seen wild deer that let people get this close.

Ashley and Katie reached Christina at the bridge. The deer stood looking at them. *What do they want?* Ashley wondered. Maybe they were hungry and were hoping to be fed. Winter could be hard on deer, and maybe there wasn't enough new vegetation for them to feed on yet. She wished she had an apple or something to offer.

The three girls stepped onto the wooden floor of the bridge. The boards creaked beneath their sneakers. When they were about four feet from the deer, the buck stomped his right hoof. Then he turned and bolted from the bridge. The doe leapt away at his side.

Christina raced behind them.

Impulsively, Ashley followed Christina's lead. Katie was right behind her, and, with her longer legs, soon overtook her.

The deer raced along the edge of the creek. Christina leaped over stones in an effort to keep up with them. Katie's arms and legs pumped as she ran full speed. Ashley found it harder to keep up, but she ran as fast as she could along the rocky water's edge, drenching her sneakers as she splashed in and out of the creek.

Panting hard, she finally caught up to Christina and Katie, who stood laboring to catch their breath by a large boulder at the water's edge. "They're gone. We lost them," Christina gasped, holding her side.

"Well, what did you expect?" Katie asked, panting. "To outrun a deer?"

"I don't know," Christina admitted breathlessly. "I just thought . . . I don't know," she trailed off uncertainly.

As she rolled the wet bottoms of her jeans into sticky cuffs, Ashley became aware of the sound of voices. A man and woman were talking nearby. She leaned on the cool, moist boulder and peered over the other side.

Her heart jumped a beat.

"Who's there?" Katie asked, coming alongside her. "Oh, my gosh," she murmured.

Standing in the rushing water, wearing hip-high

rubber boots and casting fishing lines, were a young man and a woman. "Ned and Norma," whispered Christina from behind Ashley. "In waders!"

Ashley nodded. Ned and Norma were two of the three angels they had met. Or, at least, they were the people who they'd met in the woods before.

Ned was tall and slim, with a broad forehead and a friendly expression. His sandy-blond hair was pulled pack in a ponytail, which stuck out the back of his khaki fishing hat. His hat was studded with colorful fishing lures. He wore faded jeans and a bright checked flannel shirt beneath a khaki vest.

Norma, fishing alongside him, was a tall, striking woman with strong features. She, too, was dressed in a fisherman's hat and vest over jeans and a long-sleeved T-shirt. Her straight, jet-black hair hung to her waist and fluttered freely in the gentle breeze.

Ashley had almost forgotten the shocking violet-blue color of their eyes. Ned and Norma shared the same unearthly eye color. Katie insisted it was because they were brother and sister.

Ashley wasn't so sure. *I mean, maybe they are brother and sister,* she thought now, *but those eyes are something else.*

The only one missing was delicate, blonde Edwina. Ashley recalled Edwina's amazing eyes, exactly like those of Ned and Norma. She wondered where Edwina was.

"Don't just stand there," Ned spoke pleasantly, without turning away from his fishing rod. "Come on over and say hi."

The girls stepped out from behind the boulder. Christina's expression was one of luminous joy. Katie frowned, her eyes narrow and cautious. Ashley's heart raced, as though someone had flipped a switch and set it on high speed.

Ned and Norma looked normal enough. But they were, after all . . . angels.

Weren't they?

Ned turned and smiled. "Hi, how's it been going?" he asked.

"Not great," Ashley heard herself admit. Her own words surprised her. She hadn't meant to be so frank. She didn't know Ned that well. She hardly knew him at all.

"What the problem?" he asked, still concentrating on his line.

"My parents have been fighting. They're even talking about getting divorced. And a real sweet little colt we have is sick. I'm so worried about him." The words just tumbled from her mouth, as though she was helpless to stop them.

Ned turned to her. His strange eyes looked so warm. His whole expression seemed so sympathetic and understanding. "Hmmm," he murmured. "Divorce is tough on everybody." He shook his head. "Kids have the worst time of it, no matter how brave they try to be."

Unexpectedly, hot tears sprang to Ashley's eyes. She bit her lip and tried to blink them back.

After a moment, Ashley controlled herself. Katie and Christina had walked to the far side of Ned and now stood by Norma. She was showing them how to use her fishing rod. Katie took the rod from her. Christina examined the pretty lures on Norma's hat.

They seemed so at ease now. Christina was sure she was in the presence of an angel. Katie was probably sure she wasn't. Ashley wished she could share their certainty, one way or the other. Anything was better, she felt, than her own uncertainty.

"Where's Edwina?" Ashley asked.

"In the city," Ned replied. "She had something important to do. A research project."

"What kind of research?" Ashley asked.

"Human."

"Excuse me?"

"Edwina is doing human research. She's a student of humanity," said Ned, turning back to his fishing.

"What do you mean? Statistics? Is that what she studies?"

Ned shook his head. "No. Edwina isn't interested in numbers at all. How many people are doing what at any given time never interested me, either."

"You mean she's studying psychology?" Ashley persisted.

"Something like that." Ned nodded.

Something tugged at Ned's fishing line, and he quickly reeled it in. "He's got something!" Katie cried excitedly.

At the end of Ned's line, tangled in a bunch of loose weeds, dangled a thick, wet stick.

"Would you look at that!" said Ned, smiling as happily as if he'd snagged a large bass.

Katie handed Christina Norma's fishing pole and then grabbed hold of the stick. "Be careful of the hook," Christina warned her.

Katie looked at the stick and then over at Ned with puzzled eyes. "There's no hook on the end of this," she noted quizzically.

"There's none on Norma's, either," he replied, unperturbed.

Katie grabbed the line from the other pole and yanked it in. There was nothing but a bit of tall grass wrapped around the end. "Why aren't you using hooks and bait?" Katie asked.

"Why should we?" Norma asked.

"To catch fish!" Katie cried.

"Oh, we don't want to catch fish," Norma laughed.

"Then what *do* you want to catch?" Katie asked.

"We don't want to catch anything," said Ned mildly.

"We set things free," Norma added.

"Then why are you out here—standing in the water in waders holding fishing poles?" Katie demanded.

"People seem to like fishing so much we wanted to see what it was like," Norma explained.

"But if you don't catch anything, you won't really know what it's like," Katie pointed out.

"I'm not so sure," Norma said meditatively. "I think many people really fish because it gives them an excuse to be quiet for a while, to spend some time with nature or with a friend, or just be by themselves. If they really wanted fish, they could just walk into a fish market and buy some."

"I suppose so," Katie agreed thoughtfully. She shot Ashley a slit-eyed, brow-arched look that said, *These two are really nuts!*

"I really wish they'd all try it without the hook," said

Ned, rubbing his cheek as he spoke—as if he empathized with the pain fish experienced when caught on a hook.

From nowhere a beeping sound filled the air. Norma checked her enormous black digital watch. "Time for our meeting," she reminded Ned as she poked a button silencing the alarm.

Ned reeled in his line, sighing. "I guess we'd better not be late again this time. What are we going to tell them about Edwina?"

"Maybe she'll show up," Norma said as she slogged out of the water.

Ned laughed lightly. "Edwina?" He raised his eyebrows eloquently.

"All right. Maybe she *won't* show up," Norma admitted. "I suppose we'll just have to cover for her as best we can." Norma turned to the girls. "Do you know your way out of here?" she asked.

"I think so," said Christina.

"Good," said Norma. "Well, it was nice seeing you again."

"Wait!" Ashley cried urgently. "We came to find you because . . . because I need some help."

Norma and Ned both stopped and looked at her expectantly.

Ashley felt so foolish. Why had she said that? Did she really believe they *were* angels?

"You know," she said to Ned in a small, embarrassed voice, "help with those problems I told you about."

Norma looked questioningly at Ned. "Shouldn't she talk to Edwina about that?" she asked.

Ned seemed to think this over, then nodded. "She really should."

Ashley wondered why they thought this. Was it because Edwina was a student of psychology? Or was it because she was Ashley's guardian angel?

Somehow, Ashley couldn't bring herself to ask if Edwina was her guardian angel. It sounded too . . . crazy. "When will Edwina be back?" she asked instead.

"I'm not sure," Ned said. "If we hear from her, we'll let her know you were asking for her, though."

"When will that be?" Ashley asked.

"You can never be sure with Edwina," Ned replied.

"You just hang in there," Norma said reassuringly as she and Ned began walking down the creek's edge. "I'm sure Edwina will be able to help you."

"She's bound to show up sooner or later," Ned added encouragingly as he stepped behind the boulder.

Norma followed him, and the two disappeared from sight.

The crisp, sharp sound of a cracking branch drew Ashley's attention to the forest to her left, beyond the boulder.

Two deer leapt gracefully over a fallen tree and disappeared into the trees—a young buck and a doe.

5

"I wonder why they wanted you to talk to Edwina?" Katie asked as the girls made their way through the forest, heading back toward the ranch.

"I don't know," said Ashley. "Either because she knows psychology, or because she's my guardian angel. Those are the only two things I can think of."

"Of course!" cried Christina. "That's it! Edwina *must* be your guardian angel."

"Hold on, Christina," Katie objected. "You saw those two wackos for yourself just now. How can you possibly think they're angels?"

"How can you doubt it?" Christina countered. "You saw their eyes! And they were so kind they wouldn't even hurt a fish!"

"All that tells me is they're both kooks, weirdos who happen to be related to each other," Katie insisted.

Christina shook her head forlornly. "You're just afraid to believe in them. It's too strange for you. But deep down, you know they're really angels."

"I don't believe in believing things that aren't true," Katie said emphatically. "You're just the opposite. You'll believe anything. *Especially* if it's not true," she added meanly.

"I will not!"

"Listen!" Ashley broke in. "What if Edwina *is* my angel?"

"Which she is," said Christina.

"Not," Katie tacked on.

"*Suppose* she is," Ashley rushed on. "And she's down in the city. That might explain why everything is falling apart."

"What do you mean?" Katie asked.

"My guardian angel is off doing something else. She's not taking care of me," Ashley conjectured.

"That makes total sense," Christina said.

Katie sighed loudly. "No, it doesn't. They wanted you to speak to Edwina because she's the big psych expert, the student of humanity." Katie managed to imbue each word with incredible sarcasm.

"Well," said Ashley. "Suppose *that's* true. Then it wouldn't hurt to talk to her. It would be sort of like going to a guidance counselor or something."

"You want advice from one of those nuts?" Katie demanded. "I mean, they're nice and all—kind of cool, in a way—but they're, you know, a few eggs short of a dozen. You know, the stairs don't go all the way to the top."

"They saved us once before," Christina reminded Katie. "They saved you *twice.*"

"Whatever," Katie replied with a resigned air. "But

Ashley, even if you want to see Edwina, you'll have to wait for her to get back from the city."

Ashley frowned and jammed her hands into the pockets of her jeans. "And who knows when that will be."

They walked a bit further in silence. The more Ashley thought about it, the more it seemed that Edwina must hold the answer to her problems somehow. It was a feeling more than anything else. But it was a strong feeling.

Maybe it was Ned and Norma. There was something comforting in their soft voices and calm manner. She trusted them. If they said she should talk to Edwina, she believed she should.

"I think we should go to the city and try to find her," said Ashley.

"Edwina?" Katie stared at her, aghast. "That's crazy! The city is huge. How would you find her?"

"It wouldn't hurt to try," Christina said meditatively.

"No, it wouldn't," Ashley agreed. "We'd have to wait for the weekend, though."

"We don't *have* to wait," said Katie. "We could just skip school this one time. All we do is get on the train and go. We can be back before school is even out. No one will ever know we went."

"Until the school sends a note home saying we weren't there," Ashley reminded her.

Katie frowned. "You're right. Okay, then. We'll go next Saturday."

"We?" Ashley looked at Katie searchingly. "Then you *do* think we should go look for Edwina in the city."

"No, I don't. I *still* think you're crazy." Katie replied

firmly. "But if you two are determined to go, I should be there. You guys will get hopelessly lost without me. You obviously have no idea how big the city is. There is absolutely no hope of actually finding her."

"I think we *can* find her," Christina disagreed, staring defiantly at Katie. "After all, Edwina is an *angel*, not a regular person. We really don't know how angels work. Maybe they have a range, you know, like a walkie-talkie does. If you get too far away, you can't pick up the signal anymore. Maybe all Edwina is getting from Ashley right now is static, but if Ashley gets closer to Edwina, Edwina will sense that she's near and needs some help."

"Now I've heard everything," Katie scoffed.

"One thing we *do* know is that the angels *don't* do things the way we expect," Christina pointed out. "They don't come when you call them, and then they show up at the most unexpected times, and in unexpected ways. But it seems to me that all we can do is try to find them when we need them."

"I don't know," said Ashley. "Let me think about it some more." Ashley had never been to the city. The idea of it frightened her. She knew, too, that her parents would never give her permission to go there without an adult. And she certainly couldn't ask them to take her there to search for an angel!

They were nearing the edge of the forest, and sunlight was beginning to make its way through the trees once again. Ashley had the odd feeling that she was emerging from a mysterious, ancient world back into the sunlit, everyday world she usually inhabited. She wasn't sure which world she liked better, but she definitely felt more at ease as the red wall of the stable became slowly visible.

The girls walked out of the woods and headed to the front of the stable. Mr. Kingsley was just taking another group of four out on a trail ride. Ashley waved to him, but this time he didn't even see her. His face was serious and tight as he rode past, deep in thought.

The jarring sound of a revving motorcycle filled the air. Looking down the dirt road to the main road, Ashley saw a helmeted rider in a black leather jacket zooming toward them. She knew it was Katie's cousin Mel.

Katie's parents had died in a car accident the previous fall. Now she lived with her aunt and uncle and their twenty-year-old son, Mel. "He's early," Katie grumbled. "I told him to pick me up at six."

"It's nice of him to pick you up," Ashley noted. "I guess you guys are getting along a little better."

"No," Katie disagreed. "He ignores me as much as ever. I had to pay him five dollars to come pick me up."

"What?" Ashley yelped. "That's highway robbery! And, anyway, where did you get the money?"

"Allowance," Katie replied. "Uncle Jeff and I made a deal. I would do a certain number of chores—like a ton of chores—and he would pay me almost nothing for doing them."

"Oh, well," Ashley laughed. "You always said he was cheap!"

Katie rolled her eyes. "Cheap is not the word! He's the original miser."

"I bet he's a Capricorn," Christina put in. "They tend to be frugal by nature, and if they don't keep this tendency in check it can get out of control and become cheapness."

"I don't know what he is," said Katie. "His birthday is sometime after Christmas."

"He's a Capricorn, all right," Christina said proudly.

"That's pretty good," Ashley told Christina admiringly.

"Thanks," said Christina. She turned back to Katie. "I thought you and your uncle were getting along better these days."

"We are," Katie admitted with a shrug. "He and Aunt Rainie really aren't that bad. Uncle Jeff is just cheap and kind of strict. That's all."

As they spoke, Mel came to a stop several feet away. "Got to go," said Katie. "I'll see you on Monday." Katie got on the back of Mel's motorcycle and undid the strap that fastened the extra helmet to the back. Mel never lifted his tinted visor. He just balanced the motorcycle and let the engine idle while he waited for Katie to get settled.

Ashley waved as Mel hit a pedal and sent the engine into a higher gear. He turned around in a wide circle, kicking up a cloud of dust. As she watched Katie disappear down the road, Ashley felt sorry for her all over again. "It must be horrible to lose your family," she said quietly to Christina.

"It seems like Katie's getting used to her aunt and uncle, though, and even used to Mel," Christina said.

"I suppose so. But it can't be the same as having your own family."

"I don't know," Christina mused. "If you live with people who love you, it makes a different kind of family."

Ashley shook her head. "No. It couldn't possibly be the same."

"Maybe not the same, but . . . but still good."

Ashley hoped Christina was right—for Katie's sake. Still, she was sure Katie would prefer to be with her own parents. She thought of her own parents. If they divorced, they wouldn't be dead, of course. It would be much different. But she'd have to see them separately. They wouldn't all live together anymore. Even her brothers might not live with her. It would be as if the group known as the Kingsley family had somehow died.

The Kingsley family. Ashley had never realized it before, but being part of her family had made her feel secure and safe. She'd always felt protected by the knowledge that her parents stood behind her—and they stood together, strong and unified. And even though Jeremy and Jason were often annoying, there was something about having two big brothers that made Ashley feel confident. Anyway, they weren't *always* annoying. Sometimes they were okay.

If Ashley was no longer part of the solid, strong Kingsley family, who would she be?

"I'm going to get started on my new column," Christina said, heading off toward her cabin. "Do you want to come over?"

"No, I'll be all right," Ashley answered. "I'm feeling kind of pooped. I'm going to lie down and read that stuff we're supposed to read over for English."

"Okay. See you later."

Ashley turned and looked at her house, light yellow with white shutters. A wreath of dusky-colored dried flowers hung on the door. Champ dozed on the front porch, his golden coat gleaming. Sunlight lit the roof of the porch. It made a peaceful, comforting picture. It looked like the kind of house a happy family lived in.

The family who lived in this house couldn't possibly be about to unravel, to come completely apart. It just couldn't, not when the house looked so right.

Ashley gazed around at the ranch. The grass on the rolling pasture rippled lightly in the late afternoon breeze. Horses grazed contentedly in small groups. A few of the mares were round with the foals that would be born soon. A brown split-rail fence fenced them in, but they never really tried to escape. They were happy here. This was their home. Most of them had been born here.

What would happen to them if the ranch was sold? What would happen to the horses? Would their new owner know them all by name —know their particular quirks and needs—the way Ashley and her family knew? Would they care in the same way?

Ashley went into the house and straight to her room in the hallway at the far end of the living room. She picked her pink-trimmed purple backpack off the floor. As she fished for her English literature book, she noticed that the red nail polish on her right hand was chipped in a few spots.

Putting down the pack, Ashley took a bottle of polish remover from the top of her tall white dresser and carried it to her white desk, beneath a window facing the back of the house. On the desk was a box of tissues in a white wicker cover. She pulled a tissue out and placed it under her hand. She soaked a cotton ball from a pink ceramic dish with remover and began to rub off the chipped polish.

When she was done, Ashley took a bottle of red polish from the top drawer of her desk. Carefully she laid on the new polish, paying special attention not to get any on her cuticle or the sides of her nails.

Ashley was proud of her nails. She always kept them perfectly manicured and polished. Since she helped out with the horses, this wasn't always easy. It was important to her to keep them strong and well-cared for. Ashley felt that her hands said something about who she was. Polished, put-together, attractive—that was the image she wanted to project to the world. She was the only girl she knew who actually polished her boots and ironed her jeans. That was all right. If that was what it took to look the way she wanted, then she didn't mind doing it.

Spreading the fingers of her right hand, Ashley admired the wet, gleaming red polish on her nails. She blew lightly on them to help them dry. As she was blowing, she noticed something move just outside her bedroom window.

The back of the house wasn't usually used. It was just a patch of grass with a split-rail fence separating it from the woods. There was almost never anyone back there.

Ashley leaned over her desk and parted the gauzy white eyelet curtains with her left hand. When she peered through the window, she saw her mother leaning heavily on the fence.

Mrs. Kingsley covered her face with her hands while her shoulders heaved with sobs.

6

"Are you sure?" Ashley asked a dark-haired girl named Lizzie at school the following Monday. It was a few minutes before homeroom, and their teacher, Mr. Palmero, hadn't come in yet. "Are you positive it was Trevor?"

Lizzie shook her head confidently. "Trevor was there at the movies with Rhonda Lynbrook. And they were holding hands, too."

So he wasn't sick after all, Ashley thought, slowly, hurtfully absorbing Lizzie's revelation. How could he do this to her?

Ashley looked over at Rhonda Lynbrook, sitting in the front of her homeroom class. Rhonda's light blonde hair bounced with loose curls that could only have come from hot rollers. She was very pretty but wore too much heavy mascara shading her round, blue eyes. She smiled a lot, though she rarely said anything in class. Ashley had never heard her voice an opinion or even answer a question.

Did Trevor really like Rhonda more than he liked her? He must. He'd lied to her just so he could go out with Rhonda. But why? Ashley knew she was smarter and funnier than Rhonda. Why had Trevor picked Rhonda over her? Did he think Rhonda was so much prettier than Ashley? Were looks so important to him?

She peered at Rhonda. It just didn't make sense.

Rhonda turned toward the back of the classroom and Ashley looked away quickly. "Thanks for telling me," Ashley said to Lizzie.

"I just thought you ought to know," whispered Lizzie as she took her seat, two rows behind Ashley's. "I know you've been hanging out with Trevor."

"What's the matter, Ashley?" Katie stopped at Ashley's desk as she came down the aisle.

"Trevor went to the movies with Rhonda on the night he was supposed to go with me," Ashley said very quietly. Her eyes felt achy and her nose pricked. *I can't cry now!* she thought, horrified.

Katie scowled. "That creep! You know, I didn't want to say this to you before, but I never liked the guy."

"Why not?" Ashley asked.

"I don't know. There's something annoying about him. He thinks he's too cool for words."

"Don't you think he's cute?"

"I guess," Katie admitted. "But in an annoying sort of way. His hair bugs me."

"His hair?"

"Yeah. It's too perfect on top and then his bangs flop in his eyes like he planned it that way. It's annoying."

"How can you be annoyed by someone's hair?" said

Ashley, completely forgetting her misery for a moment. "That's crazy."

Katie shrugged. "You can tell a lot about a person by his hair," she observed knowingly. "That bangs-in-the-eyes thing is totally phony, if you ask me. You can't trust anyone who thinks about their hair that much."

"You're crazy," Ashley said again with a light laugh. Telling Katie made it all seem less hurtful. Katie's opinion of Trevor's hair made it seem almost funny.

"That's why he likes Rhonda," Katie whispered. "They both adore their own hair. They'll probably exchange mirror and comb sets for Christmas."

"Stop it," Ashley giggled. "You're bad."

A boy named Darrin came in and sat between Lizzie and Ashley. "You girls will have to stop talking about me now," he kidded Katie and Ashley. Katie rolled her eyes and continued down the aisle, past Lizzie to her seat.

"Well, we *were* talking about annoying things," Ashley told him, grinning. Darrin was a pest, but he'd been a pest since first grade, so Ashley was used to him. Besides, he was interested in Katie, she thought, although Katie had indignantly rejected this idea when Ashley had suggested it.

Mr. Palmero came in, and the class quieted down. As he took attendance, Ashley sat with her chin propped on her hand, thinking about Trevor. He'd seemed to like her so much. She didn't understand why he would do this to her. Different emotions were all mixed up inside her: hurt, embarrassment, anger. Strangely, she felt that it must somehow be her fault. Had she done something, said something to change his mind? Was it the way she looked? Maybe he didn't like short girls. Rhonda was a few inches taller. Or maybe, Ashley thought, she talked too much—Rhonda hardly made a sound except to giggle or say "Really!" sometimes.

After homeroom, Ashley and Katie walked to math class together. "How's Junior?" Katie asked.

"Worse," Ashley replied.

Katie looked at Ashley with a worried expression. "It sure does seem like things are going wrong for you these days," she observed. "I always think of you as being kind of . . . I don't know . . . golden."

"What?"

Katie laughed self-consciously. "I know it sounds weird, but, you know . . . you're so pretty. You always look so pulled-together, and you have the perfect family, like on a TV show. And you live on a horse ranch. What could be cooler? Even when you get in trouble at school, the teachers act like it's kind of adorable."

Ashley had never thought of herself in exactly those terms, but she suddenly understood how it might look that way to Katie. She laughed bitterly. "Thanks. The perfect family and the ranch might all dissolve pretty soon, though. And what good is being pretty and pulled-together if I get dumped for Rhonda the airhead?"

They walked together in silence for awhile. Then Katie spoke seriously. "Do you really think this is all happening because Edwina is your angel, and she's gone?"

"I don't know," Ashley admitted. She'd never had bad luck like this before. It was more than bad luck, really. Her whole life was teetering on the brink of disaster. "I go back and forth. Sometimes I'm sure she's my angel. Other times, I just don't know. I think it's possible, though. Are you really positive there are no angels?"

Katie looked at Ashley thoughtfully. "Of course I'm not a hundred percent sure. It's not easy to believe in angels. But—you know—I saw the same thing you and Christina did."

"I know," Ashley said. "I keep wondering if it was real, though. I was sure it was, at first."

"Me, too," Katie agreed. "But when I think about it now, it seems like it couldn't possibly be true."

"I know what you mean," said Ashley. "But if it *is* true, finding Edwina might be my only hope. I heard Mom and Dad arguing in their bedroom this morning before I left for school."

"Maybe we'd better not wait to go to the city," Katie said. "This sounds like it's getting worse. You said Junior's getting worse, too."

"I know," said Ashley as they stepped into their math classroom. "Maybe you're right, we shouldn't wait."

At lunchtime they met up with Christina in the cafeteria. "I have some exciting news," she told them on line.

"What?" Ashley asked her.

"I did a tarot reading for you last night and something very interesting came up."

Ashley was surprised to feel lines of goose bumps run up and down her arms. What had Christina learned from the tarot reading?

"The death card kept coming up," Christina said with quiet excitement.

"The death card!" Ashley gasped.

"Why did you go and tell her that?" Katie berated Christina. "Doesn't she already have enough to worry about without you and your dumb, flake cards making things worse?"

"No, you don't understand. The death card can be good. It doesn't have to mean actual death, like in dying," Christina explained quickly. "It can mean the end of something—like the end of your bad luck!"

"Or like the end of a family or a ranch, or both," Ashley said miserably, her heart starting to race.

"No! Ashley, you have to think positively," Christina said. "This period of your life is coming to an end. I'm sure that's what it must mean. If I thought it was real death, well . . . well . . . I wouldn't even have told you."

"Could it mean Junior is going to die?" Ashley wondered aloud.

"Well . . . uh . . . that's one possible meaning, I suppose," Christina admitted. "Oh, I never should have told you about it!"

"That's for sure," Katie said darkly.

"I didn't think it would worry you, Ashley. I really think it means the end of bad things happening and the beginning of good things happening," Christina insisted. "But you shouldn't worry. Really I'm still just a beginner with the tarot. Maybe you should go to a professional reader."

"And maybe you should go to a psychiatrist," Katie told Christina rudely. "The death card," she scoffed. "That's like something out of cheap horror movie. The death card. Give me a break."

Christina scowled at Katie for a moment, then turned back to Ashley. Her face softened and she laid one hand on Ashley's arm. "I'm sorry, Ashley. Forget I said anything. I didn't mean to worry you. I truly don't think it's anything to worry about. It's a good thing. Honest."

Ashley nodded. "It's all right. They're just a bunch of cards, anyway." But, as she moved forward on line, Ashley felt sick inside. The cafeteria food held even less appeal than usual. She forced herself to take a dish of red gelatin. There was no way she would be able to eat anything else. All she could think about was the death card.

The death card. Tarot cards were another thing she wasn't sure she believed in. But what if it *was* true? Why did the death card have to keep coming up?

Ashley went through the rest of the day in a half-dream. She heard what her teachers were saying, yet she couldn't manage to pay attention. She kept thinking of the death card and what it could possibly mean.

When the final bell rang, Ashley rounded the hallway corner and discovered Trevor waiting for her at her locker. She inhaled sharply and fought down an urge to turn around. What did he want? Had he come by to tell her that he was now officially going out with Rhonda?

Ashley forced herself to keep walking forward to her locker. "Hello," she greeted Trevor with what she hoped was iciness in her voice.

"Hi," he said, as if nothing was wrong.

As Ashley dialed her locker combination, she realized her hands were trembling. Trevor was so cute, and he *seemed* so nice. There was something about him that made her all quivery inside. Even knowing how he'd lied, she couldn't bring herself to dislike him.

"I just wanted to say sorry again about the other night," he said, leaning against her locker. He pushed his blond bangs out of his innocent brown eyes and smiled at her. "You wouldn't believe how sick I was. It was awful."

Ashley looked up at him. How could he lie so smoothly? It seemed impossible. But what if Lizzie had been mistaken? What if she was just trying to make trouble? On TV shows there was always some girl who liked to make trouble.

"How are you feeling now?" Ashley asked.

"Better," said Trevor. He rested his hand casually on Ashley's shoulder. His touch made her heart pound. "I'd better get going, or I'll miss my bus," he said. "I just wanted to say hi and see how you were doing."

"I'm fine," said Ashley.

"See you tomorrow," Trevor said as he headed down the hall. When he was out of sight, Ashley leaned back hard against her locker door. What was going on? He *did* like her. He wouldn't have come to her locker if he didn't. Even if he *had* been out with Rhonda, there must be some good explanation. She didn't know what it could be, but it might be something really understandable.

Feeling light and happy for the first time that day, Ashley hurried for the bus. Things were going to be all right between Trevor and her. She'd been worried for nothing.

On the bus she sat with Christina as usual. She told

Christina about Trevor. "Great," Christina said sincerely. Then she took out her astrological charts and began working on them. "They want my column by the end of this week," she explained.

"Sure, go ahead, work on it," said Ashley. She gazed absently out the window as the bus drove through downtown Pine Ridge. It wasn't much of a town, just a line of low, brick shops on either side of a wide street.

Suddenly Ashley sat forward in her seat, pressing her hand against the window. A couple was going into Hanley's ice cream shop, hand in hand.

It was Trevor and Rhonda!

Ashley felt a sharp pain in her chest. She turned and watched them for as long as she could. They had definitely been holding hands! She'd seen it with her own eyes!

"What?" Christina asked, looking up from her charts.

"I saw Trevor. He was with Rhonda."

Christina leaned over to get a look, too late. She patted Ashley's back sympathetically. "Maybe he wasn't meant for you."

Ashley suddenly found Christina's philosophical attitude incredibly irritating. "Who knows who was meant for whom?" she snapped. "Are you suddenly the answer-lady of the universe? First you know that the death card doesn't really mean death. And now you know Trevor wasn't meant for me. A guy either likes you or he doesn't. It's not like it's some big mystery of the cosmos! Everything in the world is not some supernatural mystery, Christina."

Christina shot her a hurt, *what's-the-matter-with-*

you? look and settled back in her seat with her charts.

"Sorry," Ashley mumbled.

"No problem," said Christina without looking up.

They rode the rest of the way home in silence. As they got off the bus and walked up the dirt road, they didn't say much, either. Finally, just before Christina was about to turn off to go home, Ashley took her wrist. "I'm really sorry for being so crabby," she said.

"That's okay." Christina said sincerely. "I know things haven't been going too well lately. Me and my death card couldn't have helped, either. Although I really feel it's a positive sign and not a negative one."

Ashley forced a smile. "I know. It's okay. Really. You were only trying to help. I'll see you later."

"Later," Christina agreed.

Ashley continued up the road. Alice was just bringing in a group of riders. She waved to Ashley. Champ sauntered across the road from the house toward the stable. Ashley took comfort in the normal familiarity of the scene. Everything looked just the same as always. She decided to go check on Junior, but first she wanted to put her pack in the house.

As soon as she walked through the front door, Ashley heard her father's raised voice coming from the den. She froze in the front doorway and listened.

"We can't sell May, Judy!" he cried. "What would Junior do without her?"

"Hank, I don't like it, either, but Junior doesn't look like he's going to make it. I just said we can sell May *if* Junior dies!" Mrs. Kingsley replied, her voice subdued but angry.

"We're not selling May," Mr. Kingsley said stubbornly.

"All right then," Mrs. Kingsley shot back. "Which horse should we sell?"

"None of them! We are not selling any of the horses on this ranch!"

"Fine! Exactly where do you think the money we need will come from? Do you know how much we owe? We even owe Alice last week's pay!" Mrs. Kingsley said, her voice climbing higher with every word.

"Boarder horses," said Mr. Kingsley. "We'll get more boarders."

"What boarders? Mrs. Kingsley cried. "Where are you going to find them, Hank, and when? And how?" she finished weakly, near tears again, Ashley could tell.

"Would you lighten up, Judy?" Mr. Kingsley shouted.

"Would you get serious?" Mrs. Kingsley countered. "Your refusal to deal with this is the death blow to this ranch. And let me tell you something—it's about to become a death blow for our marriage, too!"

A death blow? The words hit Ashley like a punch. Christina's death card! It was coming true! And so swiftly!

At that moment, Mr. Kingsley turned and noticed Ashley standing there. He opened his mouth as if he wanted to say something, then closed it again, apparently not knowing what to say.

Mrs. Kingsley looked startled. "Everything's all right, hon," she said. "Don't worry. Just give us some privacy a minute, all right?" she muttered apologetically, shutting the French doors that separated the den from the living room.

Feeling dizzy and sickened, Ashley ran to the kitchen. She sat heavily on a chair and tried to compose herself with deep breaths. Then she grabbed up the phone and punched in Katie's number.

Katie answered. "Hello?"

"Hi, it's me, Ashley. Listen, I think we'd better go to the city."

"All right," Katie replied. "When do you want to go?"

"As soon as possible," said Ashley.

7

Tuesday morning, Ashley paced back and forth on the Pine Ridge train station platform, while Christina bounced up and down anxiously on the balls of her feet.

Getting to the station hadn't been easy. Monday night, Christina and Ashley had sneaked their bikes out to the split-rail fence near the road, where they usually met the bus. Then, in the morning, they walked out to the road as if they were getting the bus. Instead of waiting for it, though, they jumped on their bikes and pedaled the twenty minutes to Pine Ridge.

"Where's Katie?" Ashley worried, using her hand to shield against the sunlight as she scanned the parking lot next to the station.

A motorcycle roared into the parking lot. It was Katie's cousin Mel, with Katie on the back of his motorcycle. As Katie ran in to buy a ticket, Mel zoomed away.

The approaching train whistled. "Hurry up!" Ashley called to Katie. As Katie raced up the platform toward them, the train's doors whooshed open.

"Wow! Just made it!" Katie panted as she hurried onboard.

They took the face-to-face end seats, which were larger and allowed the three of them to sit together. "That was close," Ashley said, letting out a long breath as the doors shut and the train lurched into gear.

The conductor came to take tickets. "No school today?" he asked pleasantly.

"We're . . . on a research project," Ashley replied quickly.

"Oh, yeah? What are you researching?"

"Angels," Katie answered. "There's a great section on angels at the Astor branch of the library."

"Angels, huh?" the conductor said, looking interested.

"At the library."

"Are you interested in angels?" Christina asked.

The man frowned thoughtfully. "Well, in a way," he said.

"We are, too," said Christina. "Very interested. But we don't agree about whether they're real or not."

"I think they're probably real," he said. His eyes took on a faraway look, as though he were remembering some past event.

"What makes you say that?" Christina asked intently.

"Well . . . I saw an angel once," the conductor admitted, checking over his shoulder to make sure no one else was listening.

"You did?" Ashley gasped.

"Yeah," the conductor replied sheepishly as he punched their tickets. "My kid was only two at the time. Somehow he managed to toddle out onto the porch roof.

I climbed out the window after him and I was going to grab him, when suddenly he totters over the edge."

"Oh, my gosh!" Christina cried.

"Yeah, I thought I was going to have a heart attack right there, but here's the strange part," the conductor continued. "As I leapt across the roof to get him, I swear I saw this beautiful face right up there on the roof with me. Just beautiful. And when I reached my kid, he's dangling there. The edge of his shirt got stuck on the rain gutter. It all happened really fast. In another second he would have fallen, but him getting caught like that gave me the extra time I needed to grab him. And here's the kicker: guess what he says to me when I pull him back up on the roof?"

"What?" Ashley asked.

"He says, 'Lady hook me.'"

"A lady hooked him to the rain gutter?" Katie said incredulously.

"Yep," the conductor nodded. "What else could he have meant? My wife still thinks I'm crazy, but I saw what I saw, and that's what my kid said."

"We don't think you're crazy," Christina told him.

The conductor smiled. "Thanks. Hey, maybe you can use my story in your report. Like, a true-life experience."

"Good idea," Katie remarked.

"Well, good luck with your report," the conductor said as he moved on to the other passengers.

"Thanks," Ashley replied.

"See? I'm not the only one," Christina said when he was out of hearing range.

"So, that doesn't prove anything," Katie said. "That little kid just got lucky."

"But he *saw* a face," Ashley reminded Katie.

Katie shrugged. "That's how he remembers it. Who knows what he really saw or didn't see?"

Christina let out a small, frustrated cry. "You are so stubborn!" she told Katie.

"I'm not stubborn, I'm just being realistic," Katie insisted.

As the train moved sedately down the tracks, Ashley, Katie, and Christina went over their plan for the day. The trip to the city would take about an hour. They'd get there by nine-thirty, look for Edwina until one o'clock, then get a one-thirty train home. They'd be back at the station by two-thirty. They could be at school by three.

Together, they'd go to the office and explain that they were in the same car pool and had arrived late but been marked absent by mistake. The school didn't send home notices for lateness, so their parents would never have to know they hadn't been in school that day.

The trip went quickly. Soon they were pulling into the station. "The first thing we need is a newspaper," said Katie as they stepped out of the train onto the busy platform. "That will give us an idea of where to start looking."

Katie led the way, darting and weaving through the crowd. Ashley and Christina had to work hard to keep up with her. "You're good at this," Ashley commented.

"Walking through crowds is a city skill," Katie said proudly. "You country bumpkins just stick with me."

Ashley could see how happy Katie was to be back in a city. She'd lived in the city before her parents' car accident. Ashley couldn't imagine how hard it must have been—must still be—for Katie to adjust to country life. Usually Ashley and Christina were the ones showing *her* around. Now Ashley dimly realized how Katie must have felt. It was an uncomfortable feeling, not being sure of where you were or where you were going.

Ashley was glad of Katie's self-confidence in the city. Though it was exciting to her, the city was also an overwhelming place full of strangers. It was kind of frightening.

Katie stopped at a newsstand in the station lobby and picked out *The Times*. She sat on a wooden bench inside the station and quickly started thumbing through it. "I'm looking for anything that seems kind of angelic," she explained.

"Hey, how about this!" she said, excitedly pointing to an ad. "The Heavenly Arms Hotel. Maybe she's staying there."

"Do angels stay in hotels?" Christina wondered.

Katie shrugged as she refolded the paper. "Who knows? Do you have a better idea?"

At the station information desk, Katie got a free map. "The Heavenly Arms is on Third Street," Katie said as she studied the map. "It's not far from here."

Walking at a fast clip, Katie steered them toward Third Street. The Heavenly Arms turned out to be an elegant hotel with a long, red canopy overhanging the entrance. Katie boldly led them into the lobby. She rang the bell at the front desk and asked if anyone named Edwina had checked in. "Just give me all the *Edwina*s. I'm not sure what last name she's using," Katie told him.

The clerk looked at her skeptically. "And what is your relationship to this Edwina person?" he asked.

"My sister," Katie replied.

"Yet you don't know her last name?"

Ashley's heart sank. Even Katie couldn't talk her way out of this one.

Katie leaned in toward the clerk and spoke in a low, confidential tone. "She's not all there in the head. Sometimes she uses the last name Galen, sometimes Nagle—she sometimes even calls herself Edwina Angel. I can never be sure."

"I see," the clerk sniffed. He checked his computer. "Not a single Edwina," he told them. "It's not your most common name."

"Thanks, anyway," Katie said disappointedly. They headed out of the hotel.

"Now what?" Ashley asked.

"Look at this," Christina said, walking over to a pink advertisement tacked to a telephone pole. "The Pearly Gates Bed and Breakfast. That sounds sort of angelic."

Katie studied her map. "That's not far from here, either. Let's check it out."

The Pearly Gates Bed and Breakfast was a narrow brick building crammed between two larger buildings. Inside, a tiny woman with short silver hair smiled at them when they came in. "Oh, yes, Edwina," she said when they asked. "Blonde? Very pretty, an angelic face, really. Does that sound like your sister?"

"Yes!" Ashley cried. They'd found her! It was miraculous! Ashley's heart pounded with anticipation. Soon she'd be speaking to Edwina.

"That's her," Katie said. "What room is she in?"

"I'm afraid you've just missed her," the woman answered. "She checked out this morning. She said she had a modeling assignment in France."

"Modeling?" Katie cried out in surprise.

"France!" Christina gasped.

Ashley was too stunned to speak. A model? She'd thought Edwina was an angel—or a psychologist. But a model? This was an unexpected turn!

"Yes, didn't you know your sister was a fashion model?" the woman asked sweetly.

"Oh, sure we did," said Katie. "We just thought . . . uh . . . that she'd come here for a vacation. We didn't know she was working."

"Oh, yes, indeed," the woman said fondly. "She worked every day while she was here. What a lovely girl."

Slowly Ashley got over her surprise and began to think clearly again. Had the woman said Edwina was leaving the country? Leaving the country! She couldn't very well go chasing Edwina to France!

"Did she say *when* she was going to France?" Ashley asked, trying hard to keep the panic out of her voice. France! They would never find her if she went to France!

"She didn't say, dear, but it must be soon, or otherwise she wouldn't have checked out."

"Did she say where she was working?" Katie asked.

"No, I'm afraid not. Is something wrong?"

"Um . . . a . . . no," Ashley stammered. "We just wouldn't want Edwina to go to France before we have a chance to talk with her."

"Come on. We can still find her," Katie said.

"Tell her *bon voyage* for me," the woman called after them as they hurried back out through the front door.

"*Bon voyage*?" Ashley echoed when they were back out on the sidewalk. "This can't be happening! She's a model now? And she's going to France?"

"I know," Christina agreed. "I can hardly believe it, either. But if Edwina goes *bon voyage* your boat is sunk!"

8

Katie, Ashley, and Christina sat on a bench in a small, fenced-in park in the middle of a traffic circle. Sitting shoulder to shoulder, they pored through the newspaper. "Modeling agencies must be listed in here somewhere," Katie fretted.

Finally, they left the square and the went in search of a phone book. It seemed as if no public phone in this city had one, though in some they could see where the book had been. Then, they came to a booth near a bus stop with a thick yellow phone book chained to it.

Ashley picked up the heavy book and turned to a section headed *Modeling Agencies*. "There must be dozens in here," she reported glumly. "We'll never find her."

Katie joined her at the phone booth. "Let me see that." She frowned as she read through the listing. "Okay, we can handle this. We'll just check them all out."

"We can't possibly locate every one of these agencies by one-thirty," said Christina.

"We don't have to *go* to every agency. We can call," said Katie. "Altogether, how many quarters have we got? I have five."

Ashley and Christina checked their pockets. Between them, they had ten more.

"We'll call the first fifteen and ask for Edwina. Maybe we'll get lucky. If we don't, we'll go get more change," said Katie, stepping into the phone booth.

It took half an hour to make the calls. Most times a receptionist put them on hold and they waited for what felt like forever while she tried to find out if their agency employed a model named Edwina. Each time, the answer was no, no one by that name worked at the agency.

The girls had used their last quarter. "Let's go get change," Katie said. They hurried to the end of the block, where three small, charming restaurants with green awnings stood in a row. "I feel funny going in just to ask for change," said Ashley. "Maybe we should eat lunch in one of these places."

"There's no time," Katie disagreed, pulling two crumpled dollars from her back pocket. "We'll get a hot dog from a stand, later."

"Ew. Gross," Christina said, delicately wrinkling her nose.

Katie put her hands on her hips. "What's wrong with hot dogs?"

"I've been thinking lately that the consuming of a living creature seems sort of . . . well . . . mean," Christina replied.

"Hot dogs aren't living creatures!" Katie cried.

"They're made from meat, and meat comes from animals as you full well know, Katie," Christina replied firmly. "Besides, I've never liked hot dogs."

"We'll buy you a knish, then," Katie said impatiently.

"A *ka*-what?" Christina asked.

"It's this kind of potato thing," Katie tried to explain. "Sometimes they sell them at hot-dog stands. Trust me. You'll like it, unless you're also feeling sympathy for your vegetable friends these days."

"Oh, very funny," Christina scoffed. "Let's just go in and get the change."

They chose the middle restaurant, and pulled open the heavy glass front door. Potted ferns hung from the ceiling. Customers sat at tables with green cloths and white linen napkins. Katie asked the hostess who greeted them if she could have eight quarters for her two dollars. The young woman looked annoyed but went off with the money.

Ashley gazed around. To her right was a long bar at which some customers were seated, eating lunch. Most were men who ate silently as they watched a soccer match being broadcast on the television over the bar. To her left was a small dining room, and behind that was another room a few steps higher than the first room. Lovely, soft music drifted out of that room.

Lifting up on the balls of her feet to see who was playing the music, Ashley spied a large harp. The musician's back was to her, but Ashley could see she was a slim woman with long, gently waving blonde hair.

A harp!

Long blonde hair!

"Edwina!" Ashley breathed.

Excited, she hurried through the restaurant and up the three stairs to the elevated room. The musician was just finishing her piece when Ashley reached her and grabbed hold of her arm. "Edwina, I'm so glad to have found you!" she blurted out happily. "I—"

Ashley stopped short. The woman she was talking to didn't really look a thing like Edwina, not from from the front.

Hot embarrassment ran through Ashley. She was sure her face was turning bright red. "I'm so sorry," she said, backing away. "I was sure you were someone else. I'm sorry."

The woman just looked at her with a startled, puzzled expression, as though Ashley were some sort of lunatic.

Aware that people had stopped eating and talking to look at her, Ashley hurried quickly back through the restaurant. On her way, she collided with a busboy, knocking over one of the full water glasses on his tray. "Oh, gee, sorry," she said, jumping back in surprise as the water splashed her.

"No problem," he grumbled, stooping to get the glass.

Mortified, Ashley made her way back to the front entrance with her head tucked down so she wouldn't have to see any of the people staring at her. But when she reached the front of the restaurant, Katie and Christina weren't there. She peered out through the glass front door, but didn't see them on the street, either. *They must be so humiliated by me that they're hiding*, she decided.

Then she saw them, standing at the entrance to the bar section staring up at the TV, totally engrossed in whatever it was they were watching. How could they think about soccer at a time like this? Ashley wondered. Christina, especially, couldn't care less about sports!

Ashley walked over. "What are you two . . ." Ashley froze when she saw what they were watching.

It wasn't soccer.

It was a commercial for Angel Dear soap. A gorgeous blonde woman with startling violet-blue eyes stroked her cheek and said, "My skin is smooth as an angel's, thanks to Angel Dear."

"It's her, isn't it?" Ashley murmured, her eyes riveted to the face on the TV screen.

"Uh-huh," Katie nodded as the TV camera zoomed in on a pink-and-white bar of soap.

A heavyset, balding man sitting at the bar turned and spoke to them. "Do you know that young woman?"

"She's a friend of ours," said Katie. "Do you know her, too?"

"Not really. But my company is looking for someone like her to do a commercial for our computer software. My secretary called the Willow Agency just this morning to see if she's available."

"Willow!" Ashley cried. What luck! Since their list of agencies was alphabetical, Willow would have been one of the last ones they tried. Who knew how much time this chance encounter had saved?

"Let's go!" Katie urged, hurrying out.

"Wait, take my business card," the man called after them. "Ask your friend if she wants the job."

"She's not available. She's on her way to France," Christina called back to him.

Ashley and Christina were right behind Katie as they headed out to the sidewalk and scrambled down the street. "I'll call," Ashley said, getting into the booth first. Katie found the number and handed Ashley a quarter.

Ashley quickly punched in the number of the Willow Agency at the phone booth. "Hello, I need to speak with Edwina, please," she told the receptionist.

"One moment," the receptionist said, putting Ashley on hold.

"She's getting her," Ashley said excitedly to Christina and Katie.

A moment later the receptionist came back on the line. "You're looking for Edwina Galen?"

"Yes, that's her," Ashley replied.

"Who is calling, please?"

"Ashley . . . uh . . . Galen. Her sister."

There was a pause. "Well, all right. Ms. Galen is over doing a photo shoot at the Angel Soap building at twenty-five East Sixth. You can probably reach her there."

"Thanks," Ashley said, hanging up. "She's on East Sixth Street right now. Is that close by?"

"It's really close. Come on!" Katie led the way as, half running, half walking, they headed for East Sixth Street. "There it is!" Christina cried when they reached the corner of Sixth and Central Avenue. "Number twenty-five."

The Angel Soap building gleamed like a monument to cleanliness. Its front was made of glistening pink-and-white marble, sparkling glass, and shining steel. The girls hurried through a revolving glass door and entered the high-ceilinged lobby. "Can I help you girls?" asked an enormous guard in a bright red jacket.

Katie explained that they were looking for their sister, a model doing an Angel Dear soap shoot. The guard directed them to the fifteenth floor.

"Thank goodness we found her before she left for France," Ashley said as they rode the elevator up.

Everything would be all right now. She'd tell Edwina all her troubles, and Edwina would fix them, one by one. She was now so close to finding Edwina that Ashley couldn't imagine anything but success.

The elevator opened onto a hallway with thick blue carpeting. Full-color close-ups of luxurious-looking bars of soap hung on the walls. The girls went to the receptionist's desk and asked for Edwina. "Ms. Galen is in with the photographer now," the receptionist told them. "Have a seat. When the photography session is over, she'll be coming out this way."

The girls sat on a soft couch not far from the desk. "How long do you think we'll have to wait?" asked Christina, glancing anxiously at the clock on the wall. "It's almost twelve-thirty already."

Ashley shared Christina's concern. Anxious as she was to find Edwina, she also knew that if they weren't on that one-thirty train, they wouldn't be able to get back to school in time to claim they'd come in late.

"Look," Katie said in a sharp whisper. The receptionist was walking away from her desk. "This is our chance to sneak in."

"Sneak in?" Christina gasped in a whisper. "Why?"

"Because we have to find Edwina," Katie explained

impatiently. "What if the receptionist says we can't disturb her or something like that? We don't have any time to waste. Come on."

Ashley, Katie, and Christina got up and scurried down the hall, making sure to keep a good distance behind the receptionist. When she finally turned into an office and shut the door, they scurried past, darting around the nearest corner.

"We did it!" Ashley laughed breathlessly. "Now all we have to do is find Edwina."

Slowly they moved down the hallway past the open doorways of the offices. People in smart suits talked on the phones, typed at computer terminals, and walked back and forth briskly, carrying papers and looking serious. "I don't see any photographers," Christina whispered.

"Come on," said Katie.

They went through a door leading to a hallway with a black marble floor. Everything was much quieter here. Several doorways lined the hall. A young man approached them. The sleeves of his sparkling white shirt were pushed up, and he carried a large black-and-white photograph. "Are you girls here for a shoot?" he asked them.

"A what?" asked Christina.

"A photo shoot. You're models, aren't you?"

"Oh, yes," said Ashley quickly. "We're supposed to do a . . . uh . . . a shoot with Edwina Galen for Angel Dear soap, but we're not sure where to go."

"Follow me," said the young man. He led them down the hall and stopped in front of a wide wooden door.

"You girls are lucky," he said as he held the door open for them. "Edwina is going to be a supermodel. Being in an ad with her could make you famous, too."

"Great!" said Ashley with fake enthusiasm. Inside, she was beginning to feel awful pangs of doubt. What had happened to Edwina's study of humanity, or psychology, or whatever her research was about? And, if Edwina *was* an angel, how was she going to be Ashley's guardian angel and a supermodel at the same time? How could an angel be a model, anyway? Wasn't being an angel a full-time job? Why did she even want to be a model? It wasn't like she needed the money. Did angels care about fame? Were they supposed to?

Maybe this proved Edwina really wasn't an angel, after all.

They stepped into the photographer's studio, which was just a large open room with photographic equipment and changing screens scattered around.

The girls stayed close together in a shadowy corner and looked around.

Large, bright lights hung from the ceiling or stood on high, black metal poles. They were aimed at a roll of blue paper with clouds painted on it, which hung from a stand.

A man with a very fancy-looking camera hung around his neck paced back and forth impatiently in front of the paper. "Come on, Edwina, we're on a tight schedule today!" he called out.

Christina grasped Ashley's wrist excitedly. "She's here!"

At that moment Edwina stepped out from behind a

screen. She looked even more beautiful than Ashley remembered. She wore a gauzy white gown tied at the waist with a golden cord. Her thick blonde hair flowed to her waist in gentle waves. Behind her perfect features, her face glowed with an inner radiance. Her dramatic, unearthly eyes seemed lit from within.

"No! No! No!" the photographer cried. "That doesn't say angel to me at all! Lydia! Lydia!"

A young woman with maroon hair, dressed in black tights and an oversized shirt, hurried to the photographer. "Lydia, make her look more like an angel," the photographer said. "Do something with her hair. And she needs more makeup. Please, I'm in a hurry here."

"Do you believe it," Christina sighed. "That guy doesn't even know an angel when he sees the real thing."

"Maybe we should go talk to her now," Katie suggested.

"Let's try," Ashley agreed.

The girls headed across the room toward the screen where Edwina was getting changed. "Who let those kids in here?" cried the photographer.

A woman with long, straight, black hair got up from a desk and stepped in front of them. "Can I help you, girls?"

"We'd like to speak to Edwina," Ashley spoke up.

"You'll have to wait until after the shoot," the woman told them. "It shouldn't last more than another half hour. Could you please wait over there by the door."

"But it's really important," Ashley pleaded.

"Please," the young woman said firmly. "The photographer gets very upset if he's interrupted."

"It will just take one little . . . " Katie's voice dwindled off as the woman stood squarely in their path.

"Sorry," Lydia said, not sounding a bit sorry. "I'll let you know when she's free," she added pointedly.

"Oh, all right," Katie muttered. Grudgingly, the girls went back by the door. "If we don't talk to her until one o'clock, we'll never make it to the train on time," Christina said anxiously.

In a few minutes, Edwina came out from behind the screen. Her hair was piled on top of her head and it looked like it had been sprayed with red highlights. She wore a gaudy silver cape with a blue dress underneath. Her eyes and lips were heavily made-up, and her lovely complexion was hidden beneath a slathering of orange pancake makeup. Ashley thought she looked terrible. "Now *that* is an angel!" the photographer cried, pleased.

The girls looked at one another skeptically and shook their heads. "He doesn't have a clue," Christina said.

Edwina stepped in front of the blue backdrop. Lydia turned on a fan, making Edwina's clothing and hair blow behind her. Edwina struck several poses while the photographer moved around her taking pictures from different angles. "Smile, Edwina," he coaxed. "You're supposed to be an angel. Angels are happy."

Edwina smiled faintly. Ashley didn't think she looked very happy at all.

"Come on, come on, hon," the photographer insisted. "I'm not seeing angel here. Show me some angel."

Edwina's incredibly piercing eyes flashed with annoyance, but she didn't say anything. Instead, she struck another pose with arms spread wide.

The photographer took several more photos, then stopped. "Good enough," he announced. "I think I've got some pictures I can use."

Edwina nodded and walked off behind the screen.

Christina checked her watch for the hundredth time. "Look, I don't care if they throw us out, I think we've got to make one more try," she hissed. "We're dead anyway if we miss that train."

Katie looked around. Lydia the dragon lady had her back to them. "Okay, let's go," she whispered back.

The girls walked quickly toward the screen.

On the way, Ashley heard Lydia talking to the photographer. "Isn't she the most gorgeous model you've ever worked with?" she said in a voice full of awe.

"She's beautiful, all right," the photographer agreed. "But I don't think anyone will believe she's an angel. She just doesn't have the look."

What a jerk, Ashley thought. Even if Edwina wasn't an angel, she sure looked like one. Especially before they'd hidden her beauty beneath an avalanche of makeup.

As they neared the screen, they started to slow down. After all, none of them wanted to barge in on an angel while she was in her underwear or something. That would be awful! They waited awkwardly to one side.

Christina bit her lip and glanced at the clock on the wall. It was twelve-forty-five. "Don't worry. This won't take long," Ashley assured her. Once Edwina heard her troubles, Ashley felt sure she'd cancel her trip to France and come back to Pine Ridge. After all, she *was* Ashley's angel.

"What's taking her so long?" Katie worried. She knocked on the screen. "Edwina, could we talk to you? Edwina?"

Finally, Ashley couldn't stand it any longer. She peeked behind the screen.

There was no one there. Edwina was gone!

9

"What do you mean, the one-thirty train just left?" Katie asked the woman at the information booth. "It's one thirty right now!"

The woman shook her head. "It's one-thirty-three," she said primly.

"We missed it by three minutes!" Katie cried, throwing her arms in the air in frustration.

"We're dead," Christina muttered.

"When's the next train to Pine Ridge?" Ashley asked.

"Two-thirty," the woman replied after consulting her schedule.

"Definitely, totally dead," Christina moaned.

Ashley knew exactly what Christina meant. By the time they made it home, it would be too late to get to school in time to claim they'd been there all along. The school would call home to find out why they were out.

Sometimes kids got away with cutting if both their parents worked. No one would be home to take the call, and even if the office left a message, kids could erase it from the machine before their parents heard it. But Ashley's mother would be right there in the office when the call came in. She'd be sure to tell Christina's mother, too. "Is your Aunt Rainie working at the beauty shop today?" Ashley asked Katie, hoping that Katie might be spared.

Katie shook her head. "Not on Tuesdays."

The girls bought their tickets and sat silently on a bench waiting for the two-thirty train. After awhile, Katie went to a stand in the station to buy hot dogs for herself and Ashley. She got a knish for Christina. But only Katie was able to eat at all—she ate half of her dog. Christina and Ashley were too upset and depressed to eat anything.

Two-thirty finally came. The girls spent most of the trip home gazing out the window without talking. What a disaster this had been! They hadn't accomplished anything, and now they were in big trouble, besides.

Things had been going badly—but now there was not even a smidgen of hope. Edwina was *not* going to make everything better. She was a supermodel, Ashley thought glumly—not an angel, or even a psychologist.

What a waste of time! What an idiot she'd been!

The train pulled into the Pine Ridge station, and the girls got off. "How are you planning to get home?" Ashley asked Katie.

"I hadn't thought about it," Katie admitted. "Could you ride me over to Junction Hollow Road? I could probably jump on the school bus from there."

"Sure," Ashley agreed.

Christina and Ashley unchained their bikes from the

metal rack just outside the station. Katie got on the back of Ashley's bike. The girls arrived at Junction Hollow Road just as Katie's school bus approached. She hopped off and ran for the bus. "Good luck," she called to Ashley and Christina.

"You, too," Ashley replied.

Ashley and Christina rode back to the ranch. As they bumped along down the dirt road, Ashley grew more and more nervous. It was a strange feeling knowing that she was riding home to face her parents who were bound to be angry with her.

With an unhappy wave, Christina veered off toward her cabin. Ashley continued on. Goose bumps ran up her arms when she saw her mother pacing the front porch, her arms folded tightly, her face pinched in a scowl. "Where have you been, young lady?" she demanded as Ashley pulled up in front of the house.

Ashley's mind raced. Should she try a lie? A half-truth?

"I went to the city," she admitted.

"What?" her mother cried.

"I went looking for someone who could help . . ." Ashley had decided on the truth, but she just didn't know how to explain it.

"Help what, Ashley?"

Now that it came down to it. Ashley wasn't sure she could go through with this. If she told her mother the whole truth, she was afraid she'd start crying. Or, worse, that her mother would.

"To, uh, help Junior, Mom!"

"*Junior?*"

Ashley nodded, her eyes downcast. She *had* hoped that if Edwina were an angel she could miraculously cure Junior, as well as fix her parents' marriage. She'd even hoped Edwina could make Trevor like her. And maybe help save the ranch, too.

"Do you mean to tell me you went looking for a better veterinarian in the city?" her mother asked, coming down off the porch.

That *was* sort of true, Ashley thought. An angel would be the best kind of veterinarian Junior could get. "Uh-huh," she told her mother.

"And you took Christina with you?"

"Katie, too," Ashley added.

Mrs. Kingsley sighed deeply. "Ashley, we have a lot of faith in Dr. Jeffers. She's with Junior right now."

"I thought she wasn't coming back until the end of the week," Ashley said.

"She wasn't, but I called her because Junior is doing badly. She came over right away. She's an excellent vet. You know we've used her for years."

Ashley nodded.

Mrs. Kingsley looked hard at Ashley. "Ashley, you've never cut school before. What possessed you to do it now? Why did you take this on yourself? Why didn't you come talk to your father and me about it?"

Despite her best intentions, tears welled in Ashley's eyes. "I don't know, it seemed like you guys have . . . like you have enough problems right now."

That much was true, too. Her parents hadn't exactly been available lately. Even if she'd wanted to talk to them, it wouldn't have been easy. Now they always seemed to be either arguing or looking miserable and unapproachable.

Just then, Dr. Jeffers came out of the stable wearing her familiar worn barn jacket and baggy pants. She was in her early sixties and wore her gray hair short. "I have to talk to Dr. Jeffers," Mrs. Kingsley said. "Go to your room. We'll finish this conversation in a little while."

Ashley watched as her mother went off to speak with Dr. Jeffers. From the way Dr. Jeffers shook her head and frowned, Ashley guessed the news wasn't good.

She trailed miserably into the house and down the hall to her room. She suddenly saw it with new eyes, as if it were a room belonging to someone else.

What would this room tell her about the girl who lived here? she wondered.

She gazed up at the built-in bookcase at the far side of the room. The bottom shelves were lined with hardcover books, from the Winnie-the-Pooh books she'd loved as a child to the Classic Collection she'd asked for just last year, beautifully illustrated books like *Little Women*, *Jane Eyre*, and *Black Beauty*.

Above the books was her collection of dolls from around the world. She'd started collecting the dolls when she was six and had received a doll every birthday and Christmas ever since. They weren't really dolls for playing with. Each was so finely detailed. They were dolls for collecting and admiring, though, of course, Ashley did use to play with them, only very carefully. Her mother often said they'd be worth money someday.

On the shelf above the dolls was her collection of

glass figurines. She'd started collecting these in the first grade. Her first one was a small green glass turtle. For her sixth birthday she'd received a dramatic, iridescent swirling dragon on a stand of purple amethyst. Every year since then, she'd collected another.

She hadn't looked at the graceful, shimmering figurines since Christmas, when she'd been given a whimsical unicorn. But even if she didn't look at them every day, she liked knowing they were there. Most had been gifts, and each reminded her of a special event or person.

She picked up the smoky black stallion her mother had given her to celebrate the first time she'd jumped a horse over a rail, when she was eight. Holding it to the window, she admired the twisting strands of color inside.

Ashley gently put the horse back and opened her closet. Inside it was jam-packed with clothing. She loved clothes and could usually talk her mother into ordering most of the stuff she wanted from the many catalogs that arrived at the house each day. Shoes were jumbled high on the closet floor, along with leather riding boots, suede ankle boots, and several pairs of sneakers.

Sinking back onto the edge of her bed, Ashley thought about her brothers' rooms, cluttered with sports and video equipment. Jeremy loved jets and had expensive scale models hanging from every inch of his room. Jason was crazy about stock cars and had about a million books, videos, and models of them.

"The girl in this room has a lot of *stuff*," Ashley said quietly to herself. "And so do her brothers."

Her mother knocked sharply on the door and then came in. "How's Junior?" Ashley asked.

Mrs. Kingsley sat on Ashley's bed. "Dr. Jeffers isn't sure he's going to make it. We have to be prepared for the fact that he might die."

Ashley felt as if she'd just swallowed a rock. "No," she managed to say in a voice she barely recognized as being her own. "Why is this happening?" she asked. "Why is everything going so wrong?"

"Difficult, heartbreaking things happen sometimes," said her mother, and Ashley got the feeling she wasn't only talking about Junior. "Sometimes there's nothing we can do about it."

"But I used to feel like no matter what happened, someone would help me. You know, like I was never all alone. You know what? I even believed I had an angel watching over me." Ashley laughed bitterly. "A real angel. Can you believe it? I know *that's* not true anymore."

"Angels are a nice idea. I wish they *were* real. You're not alone, though. You always have Dad and me," her mother said, putting her hand tenderly on Ashley's shoulder.

Ashley bit her lip, fighting back tears. "You and Dad can't fix everything," she said in a choked voice. "You can't make Junior better. And you can't . . . you can't . . . " Her voice cracked. "You can't stop what's happening with the ranch."

Her mother looked at her with troubled surprise in her eyes.

"I heard you and Dad talking," Ashley answered her

mother's unspoken question. "Mom, are you and Dad getting divorced?"

Mrs. Kingsley looked away.

"Well, are you?" Ashley pressed.

Mrs. Kingsley laughed bitterly. "And here I thought we were shielding you kids from all this. I thought we were protecting you. I guess we haven't done a very good job." She turned back to Ashley.

Ashley returned her gaze, barely daring to breath. *Say, no,* she found herself praying silently. *Say, no, we have some problems, but we're working them out. Everything will be all right.* Ashley pinched a pucker of her lacy bedspread between her fingers and twisted it into a knot.

"It's time you knew, Ashley," said Mrs. Kingsley quietly. "Yes, your father and I are seeing a lawyer. We're getting a divorce."

10

On Saturday Ashley was busy unloading cartons from her brother Jason's old brown Chevette. She set them down one at a time on the front steps of the Pine Ridge Middle School.

In early spring the school sponsored a tag sale on the athletic field every Saturday. People who wanted to get rid of stuff that was salable paid ten dollars for a table at which they could sell things. The school got the ten dollars, and the people got to keep whatever money they made.

Ashley had never been to the tag sale before. Sometimes she'd ridden by on her bike or driven by with her mother. Although the people there usually looked pretty happy, Ashley had always felt sorry for them. She never thought she'd ever be able to part with all her precious things. Certainly not at a tag sale, where just anybody could walk up and look them over with a critical eye. She'd always felt proud, too, that she'd never owned anything secondhand. All her things were the very best, all bought brand-new.

Ashley had been grounded for the last three days, but it hadn't been so bad. It gave her time to pack up almost everything she owned and organize it for the sale. Now she was ready for the hardest part.

"Do you think you brought enough stuff, Ashley?" Jason asked snidely as he helped carry another carton to the steps.

"I brought everything I have, Jason," said Ashley, pushing a reddish curl out of her eyes. "And if you cared about our family, you'd be doing the same."

He looked into the box he was carrying. "Sorry, I don't have any dolls from around the world," he said, deliberately missing her point.

Ashley glared at him. "You know what I mean. Mom and Dad are fighting because they're running out of money, right? Why do you think they're running out of money?"

Jason shrugged as he set down the box. "Because people aren't taking trail rides as much as they used to, and the price of everything has gone up," he conjectured, running a hand through his short, red hair.

"No," Ashley disagreed firmly. "That's just part of it. It's because of us."

"Us?" Jason yelped. "You're crazy! What are you talking about?"

"I'm not crazy! Look at how much stuff the three of us have! If they hadn't spent so much money buying us everything we wanted, they'd have some savings and they wouldn't be in such a money mess. Then they wouldn't be fighting."

"Did Mom tell you that?" Jason asked as they walked back to the car together for more cartons.

"No, duh!" Ashley replied. "I just opened my eyes and figured it out for myself, genius. It was kind of a no-brainer."

"Well—duh—for your information, it's going to take more money than you can make at any school tag sale to bail them out."

Two nights before, her parents had called them all into the living room and told them about the financial mess the ranch was in. Then they'd told the boys about the divorce. Both Jeremy and Jason were completely taken by surprise. They'd had no idea.

"Your money isn't going to stop them from getting divorced, either," said Jason, lifting a cardboard box from the trunk. "Dad told me it's more than just the money."

"Like what?" Ashley challenged.

"Like . . . like . . . I don't know. He didn't say exactly. But I'm sure they wouldn't want you to sell all your stuff. If they hadn't been out this morning, they would have stopped you."

"They probably would have, but don't you see, Jason, that's the problem. They give us everything we want."

"You're crazy, Ashley. Money isn't the problem."

"Believe me, the money is a big part of it," Ashley insisted. "I figure I can make about five hundred dollars selling this stuff, and that much money would maybe pay Junior's vet bill, or feed a horse for awhile, or something. It would help, anyway. I don't see how you can just stand around and be so calm about everything. Our entire family might be broken up."

"I know, it stinks. But Jeremy and I will be going away to college in a year, anyway."

Ashley couldn't believe it. How could he be so completely self-centered? "Oh, so it doesn't matter, since you guys are leaving! Who cares about me, or Mom and Dad? That's nice, Jason! It really shows what a great guy you are!"

"I didn't mean it like that, Ashley," said Jason. "I was just saying that things will be changing, no matter what. Besides, it's not like we're going to be the only ones on earth with divorced parents."

"I can't believe you're taking this so calmly!" Ashley shouted at him.

Jason looked around, obviously embarrassed by the scene she was making right in front of the school. Other people glanced at them uncomfortably as they walked by on their way into the tag sale.

He grabbed her arm and came close to her. "I'm not calm. I hate it just as much as you do. But I'm trying to be reasonable," he whispered fiercely. "Part of growing up is understanding that there are some things you just can't change."

"Then maybe I'll never grow up!" Ashley snapped at him, yanking her arm away. She stomped off and turned her back to him stubbornly. "Oh, and don't be so sure you and Jeremy are going away to college," she said, tossing the words back over her shoulder.

"Sure we are."

"With what money?"

She turned to see his expression. He looked as if she'd just punched him in the face. She was glad. She felt like punching him in the face. "They must have saved some money for that," he said, his voice shaky.

"I wouldn't bet on it," Ashley replied coldly.

From then on, Jason seemed deep in troubled thought. He helped Ashley carry her fifteen cartons around to the back of the school, where twenty-five cafeteria tables had been dragged outside.

"Mom and Dad wouldn't want you to do this, you know," Jason said, shaking his head as he look out over the tables.

"No. That's why it was good they were out," she told him. Her parents had left the house together that morning looking grim. They'd handed Ashley a phone number, on a piece of paper and said it was where they could be reached in an emergency. Curious, Ashley had called it the moment they left.

It was a lawyer's office.

They set the cartons on the table, and Ashley paid the woman who came by to collect her ten dollars. "Can you pick me up around five?" Ashley asked Jason when the last box was on the table.

"Sure," Jason agreed. "Listen, Ashley, don't be mad. This is tough on all of us."

"Yeah, I know," Ashley mumbled. "Thanks for your help."

"No problem," Jason replied as he turned to leave.

Ashley started pulling open her cartons. First, she took out a pretty red-checked tablecloth and spread it on her table. Then, gently, lovingly, she set out her collection of dolls. After that, she put out her glass animals.

An ache formed in her chest as she looked at them.

For the first time, she had second thoughts about selling them. How could she part with them? It had taken so long to collect them. So many of them had been gifts from people who meant a lot to her.

But they were only things, after all. They weren't alive. Lovely as they were—and as much as she cherished them—they were just things. If parting with them would help her parents, then that was what she would have to do. She couldn't think of anything else that might help.

On the far end of the table, Ashley laid out the clothing. She'd held back some jeans, a few sweatshirts, a couple of T-shirts, a pair of sneakers, and her hiking boots. The rest she'd packed up for sale. Ashley ran her hand along a smooth pair of brown suede pants and sighed. They were so cool, one of the best things she owned.

With an air of grim determination, she slid them to the front of the table. Oh, well, she thought, she really didn't wear them very often. Besides, they'd been really expensive. She hoped she'd get a lot for them.

Ashley put several of her best sweaters next to the suede pants, hoping someone would come along and see how well they went together and buy the sweaters along with the pants.

As she refolded one of the sweaters, she froze.

Three tables away was Trevor!

He hadn't seen her yet. He was with his father, looking at secondhand power tools that were for sale. She remembered seeing him with Rhonda the other day. Still, her heart leapt at the sight of him.

Just then he looked up and smiled at her.

She smiled back, her heart pounding.

Ashley's fingers tightened on the sweater she held as Trevor walked over her way. She couldn't think. She couldn't move. She could only stand there with her rapidly beating heart and watch him get closer.

"Hi," he said when he reached Ashley's table.

"Hi," Ashley replied.

"Getting rid of some old junk?" Trevor asked pleasantly, eyeing her things on the table.

Ashley looked at her dolls and her glass figurines. Junk! How could he call her precious collections *junk?*

"Oh, yeah, you know," she answered shakily.

"Doing anything tomorrow?" Trevor asked.

"Uh, no."

"Want to try to do the movies again?"

Ashley wanted to ask him about Rhonda, but she just couldn't. She felt too foolish. "Sure," she replied. "I mean, I'd have to see about getting a ride to the mall."

"My dad could pick you up," Trevor offered.

"No, I can meet you," Ashley said quickly. If she was picked up, it would make it seem too much like a date. Her parents might not let her go.

Ashley wondered if Rhonda's parents allowed her to date. They probably did, she decided.

"All right," said Trevor, brushing his blond bangs from his eyes.

"Great," said Ashley. "Talk to you later."

"Later," he said, waving as he walked off.

A woman with short brown hair came by and picked up Ashley's favorite glass unicorn. "How much for this?" she asked.

"Uh . . . twenty dollars." The woman frowned and put the unicorn down. "It cost thirty-five when it was new," Ashley added.

"But it's not new now," said the woman as she walked away.

"Smile!" came a voice from behind Ashley. She turned to see Katie snapping a picture of her. "That wasn't a smile," Katie complained. "I wanted to use that picture for my article in the *Writer*. Sally asked me to come here this morning and do a photo story about the tag sale. I was really supposed to be grounded until tomorrow, but Aunt Rainie and Uncle Jeff cut my punishment short, since it was for a school thing."

"That's good," said Ashley.

"I know. But I can't use your picture unless you smile."

"I don't feel like smiling."

"Come on! It's a great day. We're not grounded anymore. And I just saw Trevor talking to you."

"You don't like Trevor," Ashley reminded her.

"Yeah, but you do."

"I know, but I wish I knew what was going on with Rhonda and him."

"Oh, who cares. She's a bubblebrain." Katie walked around the table and looked at the items Ashley had for sale. She knelt at the end of the table and took a few shots of the glass figurines. "I didn't know you were going to do this today," she said when she was done. "What made you decide to sell all this stuff?"

"Well," Ashley said slowly, trying to find the right words, "since Edwina is in France, or wherever, I figured it was up to me to try to solve my own problems."

Katie picked up the amethyst dragon and held it gently in the palm of her hand. "How is selling your favorite stuff going to help you?"

"My parents need money, and this is the fastest way I can think of to get them some. After all, they bought most of this stuff."

Katie set the glass dragon back down. "That's pretty nice of you," she said carefully. "What did lover boy have to say?"

"He wants me to go to the movies with him tomorrow," Ashley said, grateful for Katie's tact in changing the subject.

"Cool."

"Yeah, I guess," Ashley said, smiling. There was no reason she shouldn't be happy about it, but somehow she couldn't get that excited. Perhaps she just had too many other things on her mind, or maybe it was because of Rhonda.

"Christina is inside with Sally Overton, showing her the horoscope column," Katie reported.

Ashley smiled. "She worked on it the whole time she was grounded. Is it a thousand pages long?"

"Almost," Katie laughed. "She and Sally are going over it, looking for ways to cut it down, but I think Sally likes it."

"Good. I'm glad," Ashley said sincerely. Christina would have been heartbroken if Sally hadn't.

"I'd better go take a few more pictures," Katie said. "I'll be back in a little while."

"Good luck," Ashley replied.

"Same to you," Katie said with a wave as she headed toward the other tables.

A man and his young daughter approached the table next. "Daddy, I want one of those dolls," said the blonde girl, who looked about five. She pointed at the red-haired doll from Scotland, which wore a kilt and carried a bagpipe.

"How much?" asked the man.

"Uh . . . twenty dollars," said Ashley. She'd planned on asking twenty-five dollars for the dolls, but she'd decided maybe that was too high.

"How about ten?" the man offered.

Ten dollars for her Scottish doll?! There was no way she'd part with it for ten dollars! Her grandmother had paid fifty dollars for it! "Eighteen," she suggested meekly.

The man shook his head. "Sorry, hon," he told his daughter. "Let's look over at that other table. Maybe you'll find something more affordable over there."

Ashley frowned as she watched them go. Were her things really too expensive? Were these people just being cheap? Or was it that she couldn't bring herself to part with her treasures, after all?

11

By noon the tag sale was was full of people looking for bargains. Ashley had sold a vest, three T-shirts, and a pair of red leather flats, for a total of fifteen dollars.

Everyone who looked at a doll or glass figurine seemed to think it was too expensive. They didn't realize what they were really worth, thought Ashley. She considered lowering the price but she couldn't bring herself to do it.

At one o'clock, she unwrapped the peanut butter-and-jelly sandwich she'd brought along and jabbed the thin straw glued to her juice box into the box opening. Feeling discouraged, she sat cross-legged on the grass next to her table to eat her lunch.

She was almost finished when Christina arrived and plunked herself down on the grass beside her. In her hands was a thick packet of paper held together with a rubber band. "Hi. How's it going?" she asked cheerfully.

"It's *not* going—my stuff isn't going, I mean," said Ashley, offering Christina the other half of her sandwich.

Christina declined the offer with a wave of her hand

as she knelt and studied Ashley's table. "I see what you mean. It looks like you haven't sold much. How come you didn't tell me you were going to do this?"

"I don't know. Maybe I thought that if I talked about it, I might lose the nerve to do it."

Christina nodded. "I know how you feel about your figurines and your dolls. And how much you love clothes. I think you're very noble," she said sympathetically.

"Thanks." But, Ashley wondered if she *was* really noble. Maybe her prices *were* too high and she was keeping them that way because she couldn't bear to part with her things. People came to a tag sale to find bargains, not to pay a fair price for things. They wanted finds and deals, not fairness.

Christina thumbed eagerly through her stack of papers. "What you're doing is right in line with your horoscope, too," she said. "Listen to this: 'Libra is known for its sense of fairness, but nothing seems fair this month. A solar eclipse at the beginning of the month has cast a shadow over every aspect of your sign. To make things worse, combative Mars is in your house of material possessions. Yet Libra is ruled by Venus, which means love will surround you, no matter how distant it might seem at the moment. Be on the lookout for it in unexpected places.'"

"Trevor asked me to go to the movies tomorrow," Ashley told her, thinking that must qualify as love in an unexpected place.

"Great!" said Christina. "But do you *love* Trevor?"

"I don't know. But it fits into the *love* category, doesn't it?"

"It might," Christina admitted. "I don't know. Anyway, what did you think of it? I couldn't believe how much your horoscope fit you. It makes me think I'm really on the right path. Sally liked it, but she thought it was too long and too hard to understand."

"Maybe. You might want to simplify the words a little," Ashley agreed.

"I guess," said Christina. "That's what Sally said." She looked at Ashley a moment and then scanned her article. "What struck me most about your horoscope is that Mars is affecting your relations to material things. Mars usually signifies war or struggle, and here you are doing this totally extreme, difficult thing by trying to sell all your stuff. It's like the war about material things is going on inside you. Don't you think that's super-interesting? I sure do."

"*Trying* to sell is the right way to say it," Ashley said with a glum chuckle, "trying and not succeeding."

Just then, a woman dressed in slacks and scuffed boots stood in front of Ashley. Looking up, Ashley saw she was probably in her late fifties. Her frizzled black-and-gray hair hung in one thick braid over her right shoulder, and a gray, silver, and black wool poncho was wrapped around her shoulders. "Are you in charge of this table?" she asked Ashley in a husky, warm voice. She looked eccentric—but nice.

Ashley and Christina quickly got to their feet. "Yes, this is my table," said Ashley, brushing grass from her pants.

The woman inspected a black-haired doll dressed in a traditional Spanish costume wearing a black mantilla veil on her head. "How lovely!" she said. "This is your doll?"

"All this is mine," Ashley offered eagerly. Then and there, she decided that she would force herself to make a deal if that was what she had to do to make a sale happen.

"People seem to think I'm asking too much money for my stuff, but I really do want to sell it," she told the woman. "So if you're interested, we can discuss the price. I mean, I could suggest a price and if you don't like it, you could offer me a lower price. Isn't that how it's done?"

The woman barely seemed to be listening. "Mmmm-hmmm," she said with a nod as she looked over the glass figurines with intense interest. "Fine."

Ashley watched her anxiously, hoping she would want to buy at least one thing. As she watched, Ashley realized that she had the impression that the woman was very beautiful, and yet her features were plain and a bit wrinkled. She wore no makeup. Her hair and clothing weren't stylish or well-cared for. Still, the impression of beauty was so strong.

Ashley darted a glance at the woman's hands and saw that her nails were unpolished and clipped short. But she had strong hands, and she seemed to hold everything she picked up with a tender assurance. Ashley couldn't picture her ever fumbling or dropping anything.

Suddenly, the woman looked up. Ashley averted her eyes, embarrassed that she'd been caught staring so rudely.

"I'll take everything," the woman said.

"Everything?" Ashley gasped.

"How does a thousand dollars sound?"

Ashley felt as if someone had just hit her in the chest with a hardball. A thousand dollars! It was more than she'd ever imagined earning. She opened her mouth to speak but the words wouldn't come out.

"She thinks it sounds great," Christina spoke up for her.

"Wonderful," the woman said, taking a hand-stitched leather wallet from the front pocket of her poncho. She took out ten crisp hundred-dollar bills and handed them to Ashley. Then she turned and looked over her shoulder. "Leonard!" she called. "Leonard!"

A skinny young man in his twenties with short blond hair and wire-rimmed glasses hurried over from several tables away. "Yes, Ms. Elgan," he said.

"Could you please get some boxes from the van so we can pack up these items? I think they'll be perfect for our set, don't you?"

"I have cartons," Ashley volunteered, pulling out the boxes she'd stashed beneath the table.

"Thanks," Leonard said. Immediately he began gently wrapping the figurines and dolls in the crumpled tissue paper Ashley had left inside some of the boxes.

"We're filming a commercial, and I need things that look like they belong in a young girl's room. I also need clothing for the actress to wear. These items will be perfect," Ms. Elgan explained.

"Oh, I'm so glad," said Ashley.

Ms. Elgan looked at Ashley with a soft expression full of sympathy. "It must be hard for you to part with these things," she said.

"Yes, but . . . I have to do it," Ashley said. There was something in the woman's kind eyes that made her suddenly feel like weeping.

"All done," Leonard announced, closing the last of the boxes.

Ms. Elgan took Ashley's hand and pressed it firmly, affectionately. Ashley had been right. She did have strong hands. "Thank you, dear," she said. "Whatever it is you plan to do with this money, I hope it makes you happy."

"I think it will," Ashley replied.

"Good."

"Hey! I need a picture of this!" Katie cried, running across the grass toward them. She arrived at the table, panting. "I can't believe you sold everything! Could you all crowd around the boxes?"

Ashley, Ms. Elgan, and Leonard stood in front of their pile of cartons. Christina stepped away. "No, get in the picture," Katie told her. "You were here when the big sale was made."

Christina stood next to Ashley, slightly in front of Ms. Elgan and Leonard. Katie snapped several pictures of the group. "This will be a perfect ending for my article," she said happily.

When the photos were taken, the girls helped bring the cartons to Ms. Elgan's silver van. "Thanks, again," said Ashley as Ms. Elgan got behind the wheel of the driver's seat.

"Thank *you*, dear, these are just the things I needed."

The girls waved as the van pulled away. "Aunt Rainie is coming to pick me up soon," said Katie. "Do you guys need a lift?"

"That would be great," said Ashley. "Jason wasn't planning to come back for me until five. I don't feel like hanging around until then."

They sat down at the base of a spreading maple in front of the brick school. In five minutes Aunt Rainie's rust-splotched blue Chevy came puffing up the hill and pulled up in front of the school.

Katie walked over to talk to Aunt Rainie, a plump, pleasant-looking woman with a halo of frizzy blonde hair around her face. Aunt Rainie nodded and waved for Christina and Ashley to get in the car.

"You made *how* much?" Aunt Rainie gasped when they told her about Ashley's big sale.

"One thousand," Katie repeated.

"Well, what do you know. Katie, we have to look around that barn and see what stuff we can scrape up to sell. That's more than I make in a month down at the beauty shop."

"Ashley sold all her best stuff," Katie pointed out.

"She did?" cried Aunt Rainie, impressed. "Isn't that wonderful! What do you plan to do with all that cash?"

Ashley wasn't sure she should lay out all her parents' problems for Aunt Rainie. She didn't know her very well, and Mrs. Kingsley always said family business should remain private. "We have some things we need around the ranch," she said.

"Why, aren't you a treasure, pitching in like that!" Aunt Rainie gushed.

Katie turned around from her front seat and glared at Ashley in the back. Ashley knew why she was annoyed. Katie's Uncle Jeff was always complaining about bills, and ever since Katie came to live in Pine Ridge, he'd often managed to imply that she was nothing but an added expense.

"I had way too much stuff," Ashley tried to make the situation better. "I just looked around one day and said to myself, 'Boy, am I ever spoiled!' Not many girls have as much stuff as I had."

Katie looked at her and grinned, nodding her head. Now, at least, Aunt Rainie and Uncle Jeff wouldn't expect her to do the same.

"You can just drop us here," Ashley told Aunt Rainie when they came to the barn with the Pine Manor Ranch sign on it. "This is where the bus drops us. Thanks a lot."

They got out of the car, said good-bye, and headed down the dirt road. "Your parents are going to be so thrilled," said Christina. "I bet they'll say to each other, 'See, we can make this work,' and everything will start to look better to them."

"Do you really think so?" Ashley asked hopefully.

"I do. Things are looking up today. Trevor asked you out. You made an incredible amount of money. Next, your parents are going to forget all about getting divorced."

Ashley hoped Christina's hunch-power was on target today.

"I have to work on my column," Christina said when they got to her cabin. "I'll see you later."

"Later," Ashley said with a wave. She continued on to her house. By the stable, Alice was helping a group of riders mount for a trail ride. Jeremy was already on May. On Saturdays, he and Jason helped with the trail rides.

When she stepped onto the porch, she noticed her parents' Jeep parked on the side of the house. Good, they were home.

Champ looked up lazily from his spot by the door. She scratched the golden hair between his ears and he licked her hand affectionately.

With a soft smile, Ashley gazed around. The ranch was a wonderful place to live. It wasn't going to crumble, after all. She felt it deep inside, and she was proud of herself for doing her part to keep it all together. She took the ten crisp hundred-dollar bills from her front pocket. She couldn't wait to see her parents' expressions of gratitude and relief when she handed them over.

She opened the door and stepped into the living room. Immediately, she was hit with the sound of angry voices coming from the den.

"All right, Judy, have it your way! We'll sell May if Junior doesn't pull through. Will that make you happy?" Mr. Kingsley spoke harshly.

Mrs. Kingsley laughed scornfully. "You just don't get it, Hank! None of this makes me happy. Selling May is just a start. We need a lot more money than May will bring. What do you think we could get for her, at the most—seven hundred, a thousand dollars? If we sell May, that might get us through another week. That's all. Ten thousand dollars *might* begin to make a dent! And where are we going to get that?"

Biting her lower lip, Ashley folded the bills and stuck them back in her pocket.

Suddenly a thousand dollars didn't seem like very much money at all.

12

"Mom and I are going to the mall today," Christina told Ashley the next day, Sunday, as they walked toward the stable. "We can drop you off there. I already asked Mom."

"Great," Ashley said with a smile. "I can probably get a ride home with one of the kids."

Ashley pushed open the wooden door, and they stepped into the cool, shadowy stable with its rich smells of hay and horses. They went to Junior's stall and found him still lying in the hay. From the adjacent stall, May kept watch over her ailing child.

The girls entered Junior's stall and knelt beside him. Ashley batted away the flies buzzing around the listless colt, while Christina stroked his mane. He whinnied at them faintly. "That medicine isn't doing him any good at all," Christina observed unhappily.

At that moment Alice came into the stable. "Are you girls ready to go?"

"I have to go tell my parents," said Ashley, getting to her feet.

"That's all right. I just saw your mother," Alice said, looking down sadly at Junior. "She knows we're leaving."

The girls followed Alice out of the barn. "Do I look all right?" Ashley asked Christina.

"Yeah, You look fine."

Ashley pulled at the neckline of her plain navy blue sweatshirt. She ran her palms down the front of her jeans. "Maybe I shouldn't have sold *all* my clothes," she fretted. "I probably should have kept at least one pair of boots."

"You did a really nice thing," Christina assured her. "Don't worry. You look terrific. You always do."

Ashley hoped Trevor agreed. This morning she'd decided on at least six different outfits to wear today, only to remember one by one that each had been sold.

"What did your parents say when you gave them the money?" Christina asked.

"I didn't," Ashley admitted.

"Why not?"

Ashley told her about the conversation she'd overhead. "I felt dumb giving them a thousand dollars when Mom said ten thousand might not even make a difference. So I'm hanging on to it for now. I'll come up with something else to do with it, I hope."

"I bet if you gave it to them, they'd appreciate what you did," said Christina.

"I guess. But I'd feel dumb."

They climbed into Alice's brown pickup truck and bumped down the dirt road. The biggest mall in the area, the only one with a movie theater, was over in Miller's Creek, a little over a half hour away.

After they arrived and parked, Ashley said good-bye to Alice and Christina at the fountain by the front entrance. Excited, yet anxious, she headed over to the triplex. Right away she saw Trevor out front with a group of friends, other eighth-graders she knew only slightly.

As she approached, Trevor caught sight of her and smiled. But she noticed that his smile faded as she got closer. "Hi," he said, looking confused.

Ashley was suddenly very conscious of her plain outfit. The other girls in the group were dressed well. One wore a pleated blue baby-doll-style dress with over-the-knee socks and short boots. Another wore leggings and a long, fuzzy pink sweater. A third girl, like Ashley, had on jeans, but hers were designer jeans and looked great with the short red military-style jacket she wore over a ribbed sweater.

Ashley longed for her suede pants and at least one of the sweaters that went with them. Why did she have to go so crazy and sell *everything?*

"Ashley lives on a horse ranch," Trevor told the others, as if he were trying to explain her appearance.

"How cool," said one of the girls. "I guess you were out riding this morning."

"Uh . . . yeah," Ashley lied. "I didn't realize how late it was getting so I had to rush right over."

"We'd better get on line," said one of the boys. "*Wipeout Artist* is starting soon."

"We're seeing *Wipeout Artist*?" Ashley questioned, wrinkling her nose in distaste. As far as she knew, the movie was about a guy who saved the world by blowing up a building almost every fifteen minutes. Even Jeremy and Jason hadn't liked it, and they usually loved garbage like that.

"That's what everyone decided on," Trevor told her as they got on line.

"Isn't that R-rated? No one under seventeen?" Ashley objected.

"We look old enough," Trevor assured her.

"*Some* of us do," the girl in the pleated dress giggled.

Ashley glared at her. The girl looked away. *I'd look old enough if I had my regular clothes*, she thought indignantly.

When they got to the ticket window, the woman behind the booth sold tickets to all the rest of the kids, but when she got to Ashley, she asked, "Can I see some identification, please?"

"Gee . . . uh . . . " Ashley stammered. "I didn't drive today. I left my license home."

"Do you have anything? A school ID?" the woman asked.

"No, I left that home, too."

"I'm sorry, but you look too young to me," said the woman. "I can't sell you a ticket without identification."

Ashley knew she must be bright red, which only added to her embarrassment. "Maybe we could see a different movie?" she said meekly to Trevor and his friends.

"What do you suggest?" the girl in the pink sweater asked snidely. "There's an animated feature in theater two."

"You guys go ahead," said Trevor, brushing his bangs out of his eyes. "Ashley and I will see something else. Catch you later."

"I'm sorry," she apologized as they left the line and walked over to a nearby bench.

"It's okay," he said, though he sounded disappointed.

They sat side by side on the bench for several minutes without talking. Ashley just couldn't think of anything to say. "Want to get something to eat?" she suggested. "My treat." She'd brought along fifty of the dollars she'd earned at the tag sale, just in case she needed money.

"I'm not really hungry," said Trevor. She could tell he wasn't in a good mood. Was it because of the movie? Or was it because of the way she looked? He'd probably wanted to show off his cute-looking date to his friends, and she'd arrived wearing such plain clothes.

"I sold most of my things at the tag sale," she told him. "I want to buy all new stuff, but I haven't had the chance yet."

"Oh, wow!" he laughed. He seemed relieved. "Is that why you look that way? I was wondering. Man, I didn't know what to think."

"I don't look *that* bad, do I?"

"Not *that* bad, but one of the things I've always liked about you is the way you dress," he told her. "I like a girl who knows how to make herself look great. That's really important to me. I mean, how can you be a cool guy if you don't go out with cool-looking girls?"

"Girls?" Ashley asked, a sinking feeling beginning in the pit of her stomach.

"Ladies, women, whatever," he amended, not understanding what she objected to.

"So, I guess you weren't too happy when I showed up looking like this," she said.

"Sort of. Yeah."

Ashley remembered the fifty dollars in her pocket. For that amount of money, she could put together a great-looking outfit in no time. "You wait here," she told Trevor. "I'll be back in fifteen minutes, and I'll look a lot better. Your friends won't believe I'm the same person."

"Cool," said Trevor, sitting back on the bench looking pleased.

Ashley ran to a set of stairs leading to the upper level of the mall. She knew where there was an adorable clothing shop with a great line of the petite sizes that fit her best. Right next door was an inexpensive shoe store. It wouldn't take long to transform herself.

As she dashed to the far end of the mall, she slowed a bit near the pet store. She could never resist taking a glance at the puppies in the wire mesh cages up front. By the front register of the pet store, across from the puppy cages, she saw Ms. Elgan.

The woman looked up and smiled at Ashley. Ashley stopped, not quite sure why. Something about Ms. Elgan interested her. She looked the same as she had the day before, with her poncho and her gray-and-black hair in a thick braid. At that moment she was buying two gray doves in a white cage.

Ms. Elgan stepped out of the pet store. "Hello, Ashley. Nice to see you," she said. "I was just inside talking to the owners about renting some dogs for a dog-food commercial I'm working on. I couldn't resist buying these doves while I was in there."

"They're cute," said Ashley, looking at the doves.

"Are you here by yourself?" Ms. Elgan asked.

"No, I'm with a friend. He's downstairs waiting for me."

"Well, it was nice to see you again, Ashley."

"You, too," said Ashley as she began walking toward the dress shop. She was just outside the store when Ashley stopped cold.

Why hadn't she thought of it before?

Ms. Elgan made commercials!

What better way to get business for the ranch than to advertise?!

"Ms. Elgan!" Ashley called as she turned and raced back toward the pet store. "Ms. Elgan! Wait!"

Ms. Elgan was about to step into a department store when Ashley caught up to her. "I need to talk to you," Ashley panted.

"What is it, dear?"

"How much would it cost to make a commercial?" she asked breathlessly. "I mean, make one and run it on TV?"

"That depends. Are you the one who wants to make a commercial?"

"Yes. For my family's ranch."

"Well," she considered. "I could offer you a short spot on a local cable channel for fifteen hundred dollars. That's not my usual price, but I like you, Ashley."

"Fifteen hundred?" Ashley repeated, disappointed. "You wouldn't do it for a thousand, would you?"

Ms. Elgan looked thoughtful. "If you write the script, I'll do it."

"All right!" Ashley cried. "Thank you so much. Where do we start?"

"We could discuss it now, but what about your friend?"

"I'll go get him," Ashley said excitedly. "Do you mind waiting? I'll be right back."

"Not at all."

Ashley raced back toward the stairway she'd come up. Trevor would just have to understand that she couldn't buy new clothes today. She needed every penny she had to pay for the commercial. Besides, wasn't a person supposed to like you for who you were, not for the kind of clothes you had?

Halfway down the stairs she spotted Trevor. But he wasn't alone.

Rhonda and a friend of hers were sitting on the bench next to him.

Trevor was telling a joke or a story that had Rhonda and her friend in gales of laughter. Rhonda reached over and took Trevor's hand. She didn't let go, even after the laughter subsided.

Ashley took a step back up. She wasn't sure what to do. Before she could decide, Trevor got up from the bench, still holding Rhonda's hand. Together with Rhonda's girlfriend, they headed for the movie theater.

Ashley held tight to the railing. He hadn't even waited for her to come back! What if she'd returned with a whole new outfit, and he wasn't even there waiting for her? What a fool she would have felt like!

Stunned, Ashley walked slowly back up the stairs. "Is everything all right?" asked Ms. Elgan, who was waiting at the top of the stairs.

"Yes. I think so," Ashley said slowly, still trying to make sense of what Trevor had done.

The doves in Ms. Elgan's cage flapped against the bars. "Would you mind if I do one thing before we discuss the commercial?" she asked Ashley.

"No, I guess not," Ashley said. "Want me to wait here?"

"No, you can come." Ms. Elgan walked back to the department store she'd been about to enter. Ashley assumed she would buy something or other, maybe for a commercial she was working on. But Ms. Elgan led her through the store toward a set of swinging double doors, to a room with lockers, a soda machine, and tables. A sign on the wall said: 'Employees Only'. It was the room where the employees took their breaks.

"Uh . . . are you sure it's okay for us to be here?" Ashley asked.

"It's all right," Ms. Elgan assured her. "We're just passing through." At the back of the room was another door, and behind it was a set of stairs. Ashley followed Ms. Elgan up.

At the top of the stairs, they stepped out onto the flat roof of the mall. It was breezy, and Ashley wrapped her arms around herself for warmth. "What are we doing up here?" she asked.

Ms. Elgan just smiled as she set down her bird cage. "Most pet-store birds are tropical," she told Ashley. "They've been removed from their natural environment and have to stay in cages. But these doves can survive nicely in the wild in this part of the country. Right here."

Ashley looked at her quizzically. Why was she talking about this?

Ms. Elgan knelt, opened the cage, and lifted out one of the birds. It perched on her finger. "These two were due to have their wings clipped again. I got them just in time."

She reached in and took out the other one. It immediately fluttered up to her shoulder.

Ms. Elgan took the dove from her shoulder and tossed it into the air. With a wild flapping of wings, it began to fly. The second bird took off after it.

Ashley looked at Ms. Elgan, her eyes wide with surprise. She'd bought the birds just to set them free!

Ms. Elgan turned to Ashley. Her face was radiant with happiness. "I love to do that," she said with laughter in her voice.

Ashley felt a smile cross her face, a smile so wide it seemed to stretch her whole body. It seemed like years since she'd felt so light.

13

"Pine Manor horses, your best riding sources!" Katie quipped the next day at lunch. Ashley had told Katie and Christina about the deal she'd made with Ms. Elgan. Now they were busy trying to help her write her script.

"Oh, that's terrible," said Christina, shaking her head as she nibbled at her homemade beansprout-and-tofu sandwich.

"Well, let's hear you do better," Katie challenged them, picking up her hamburger and taking a huge bite.

Christina looked up thoughtfully. "Pine Manor Ranch. Feel the power."

"What power?" Katie cried.

"You know there's something mystical about those woods. The power spots."

Katie rolled her eyes. "Oh, right, right," she muttered.

"They have a tremendous concentration of energy in them," Christina reminded them.

"Yeah, like people will really believe that," Katie scoffed.

"People *do* like the powerful feeling of being on a horse," Ashley said meditatively. "When you're riding a really good horse, it's like you become part of that horse. It *is* a great feeling. How about Come to the Pine Manor Ranch. Feel the horse force and have the ride of your dreams?"

"I like it," said Christina.

"Not bad," Katie agreed. "I don't know about that 'horse force' stuff, but most commercials don't make a whole lot of sense, anyway."

"I could come out and say that stuff," Ashley speculated, "and then we could show some pictures of the ranch—except I don't have any."

"I can come over today and take some," Katie offered.

"Great!" Ashley said. "I'd have to think of some more stuff to say while the pictures are being shown. It might help if I looked at some ads."

She searched through her pile of notebooks. "My new issue of *Cool Fool* just came. Maybe there are some good ads."

As she pulled the magazine from her stack, a paper sailed out onto the floor. Christina reached down to pick it up. "Ashley, you got a D?" she gasped.

Ashley took the paper from her. "I can't seem to pay attention lately. I have too much on my mind."

"But you only get A's and B's," Christina objected.

"So? Everyone's entitled to a few bad marks once in a-while," Ashley snapped. She wasn't being entirely truthful. Lately she'd gotten more than a few C's and D's. School just didn't seem important ever since her world had started crumbling around her. "Could we get back to the ad?" she asked, tucking the math quiz into her notebook.

Ashley thumbed through the magazine. Lots of beautiful teens in gorgeous clothing smiled out at her from the ads. They looked so breezy, as though they didn't have a care in the world. "These girls all look so happy," she said quietly.

"Of course they do," said Katie. "Nobody wants to buy stuff from depressed teenagers."

"Maybe they really *are* happy," Ashley considered. "Why shouldn't they be? They're models. They're beautiful and get to wear great clothes. Everyone admires them."

"Oh, they have problems the same as everybody," Katie said, as if somehow she knew for sure.

Ashley wondered, though. How could these happy, gorgeous girls be anything other than what they appeared?

Ashley stopped turning pages at an ad for a tropical vacation resort. "Get away to a place where life is simple, the breezes are cool, and the waters are divine," she read expressively.

"Divine waters?" Katie snorted, with an impish glance at Christina. "What have they got, power spots in them?"

"They might," Christina insisted seriously.

"Puh-lease," Katie said.

"This is the kind of stuff that convinces people to go to this place," Ashley said. "You might think it's dumb, but here it is in a national magazine."

"See if you can find something better," Katie suggested.

Ashley turned the page and gasped sharply. "Look!"

She slid the magazine over to Ashley and Christina so they could see the full-color ad for Angel Dear soap—featuring Edwina. It was one of the pictures that had been taken in the studio the day they'd been there.

"Are you sure this is Edwina?" asked Christina, scrutinizing the photo.

"Sure it is," said Ashley, but she looked more closely. To tell the truth, she wasn't absolutely positive. With all that makeup, the woman could have been any pretty model.

"It looks like they did something to the photo," Katie observed as she stared at the ad. "You know, like they airbrushed it or something."

"Is that how they take out anything they don't like?" Ashley asked.

"Yeah, like wrinkles or freckles or messy hair," Katie answered. "I think they changed her face."

"But she has a perfect face," Ashley said.

"Who knows what they thought?" Christina said. "That photographer didn't even think she looked like an angel."

Something about Edwina's face *was* different. It did look as though it had been altered somehow, and in the process some of Edwina's inner beauty had been lost.

Suddenly, Ashley didn't want to look at the ad anymore. Inexplicably, it made her uneasy. "Let's eat," she said, shutting the magazine. "I'll finish writing the script tonight. Can you guys come with me to the studio tomorrow after school?"

"I can," said Katie.

"Me, too," Christina agreed. "If you want, you can

wear my fringed vest and that cowboy hat I never wear."

"Great," said Ashley. "I don't have anything left to wear."

"But you *do* have the money to pay for the commercial," Katie reminded her. "Do your parents know you're doing this?"

Ashley shook her head. Her parents were so preoccupied that her mom hadn't even noticed that anything was missing from Ashley's room. "I want to surprise them," she responded.

"They'll be surprised all right," Christina said.

Just then, Trevor walked by, holding hands with Rhonda. The two didn't notice—or pretended they didn't notice—the three girls.

"I can't believe he just left you in the mall," Katie hissed. Ashley had told them what happened before homeroom that morning. "What a creep!"

"I ran into him after I talked to you guys this morning," Ashley reported. "He said he didn't think I was coming back. He tried to lie and say he'd waited a lot longer than he had."

"That guy is a big liar," said Katie. "He lies all the time. He's been lying to you from the beginning."

Ashley nodded. "I think he couldn't make up his mind who he liked better, but then when I didn't fit his picture and Rhonda did, he finally decided."

"Who needs him?" said Christina loyally. "Good riddance."

"Yeah," Ashley agreed. But as she watched him take a seat beside Rhonda at a table, she had to admit to herself that it hurt.

* * *

That afternoon, Katie took the bus to the ranch with Ashley and Christina. She shot three rolls of film. Ashley posed next to some of the horses, smiling widely, trying to look like the happy models in the magazines. Christina demonstrated some beginner jumps she was learning from her mother. Then they posed in front of the stable. "Is there anything else I should get a shot of?" Katie asked.

"How about one of the trails?" Ashley suggested.

They walked into the woods and took some shots of the most popular trail. "What's that building back there?" Katie asked, pointing toward a rambling brown wooden building only barely noticeable through the trees.

"That's just empty," Ashley told her. "When my grandfather owned the ranch, it was a dude ranch, you know, with people staying overnight. That's the bunkhouse, but it's been shut down for years."

Katie took a picture of it through the trees. "It makes sort of a nice picture," she said.

The next day, after school, the girls took the school bus downtown. First, they picked up the photos. Katie insisted on paying, despite Ashley's protests. From there, they got on a public bus, which carried them to a stop two blocks away from the Twin County Cable Studios, where Ms. Elgan had told Ashley to meet her.

"I'm sort of nervous," Ashley admitted as they walked through the door of the low brick building.

"You'll be fine," Christina assured her with a pat on the shoulder.

They hadn't been in the lobby a minute before Leonard hurried down the hall toward them. There didn't seem to be anyone else working in the building, maybe because it was so late in the afternoon. "Hi, girls. Come this way." They followed him down a hall to a small studio. Bright blue tape *X*s marked the floor in front of a roll of paper on a stand, like the one Ashley had seen at the photographer's studio in the city. A large video camera on a huge tripod sat in the corner of the room.

Ms. Elgan was pulling down shades when they came in. Her hair fell loose down her back and was pushed off her face with a black headband. She wore a sweatshirt which had "Save the Whales" written on it, and baggy jeans. "Hi, there," she greeted them warmly. "Are you all set for this?"

Ashley explained what she'd planned for the commercial and gave Ms. Elgan Katie's photos. "Nice work," said Ms. Elgan, thumbing through them. "All right, Ashley, you stand on that blue mark in front of the paper. We'll see what we can come up with."

Christina handed Ashley the cowboy hat and fringed vest. Ashley put them on and stepped on the blue mark in front of the paper. She took a deep breath and one last glance at her script.

"Ready on the set?" Ms. Elgan called from behind the camera.

"Ready," Ashley said, tossing the script to the floor.

"Rolling," Ms. Elgan said.

Ashley pulled back her shoulders and lifted her chin. She lifted the sides of her mouth into the perkiest smile she could manage. "Hi there, dudes and dudettes," she spoke in a cheerful voice. "I'm here to tell you about the Pine Manor Ranch. If you're aching for some fine horses in a fabulous country setting, you couldn't ask for more. My family and I will be there to personally guarantee your happiness." Ashley took off her cowgirl hat and waved it to the side. "Come to where life is simple and the horses are divine. Now, let's take a look at these fantastic pictures of our ranch."

She looked at Ms. Elgan as she stepped off the blue tape. "I thought we could show the photos here and I'd say stuff along with it."

Ms. Elgan stepped out from behind the camera. "My goodness, Ashley, I would hardly have known you in that commercial. You seemed so different."

"Well, I wanted to seem . . . you know . . . full of pep."

"I see," Ms. Elgan said, nodding. "You *did* have a lot of pep."

"Was I all right?"

"We'll see how it looks when we play it back," Ms. Elgan replied. Ashley had the feeling she hadn't thought much of her performance. "Let's tape your voiceover. While we're doing that, Leonard can edit in the photos."

Ms. Elgan led the girls down the hall to a room filled with machines and dials. Christina and Ashley settled into chairs in the corner. Ms. Elgan directed Ashley to a stool under an overhanging microphone and told her to start talking when she pointed at her. She assigned Katie to hold up each photo that they'd be using so Ashley would know what she was supposed to be talking about.

At Ms. Elgan's signal, Ashley began talking. On index cards, she'd written a short speech, explaining each picture. As she spoke, though, she had the feeling that what she'd written was boring. She hoped she was wrong.

"Come to the Pine Manor Ranch," she ended her talk. "Feel the horse force and have the ride of your dreams."

Ashley looked at Ms. Elgan. "That's it," she said. "What did you think?"

Before Ms. Elgan could reply, Leonard popped his head in. "That pizza you ordered is here, Ms. Elgan," he said.

Ms. Elgan turned to Christina and Katie. "Why don't you girls go with Leonard and have a bite to eat," she suggested pleasantly. "I want to go over a few things with Ashley."

"All right," Katie agreed as Christina and she headed for the door.

"We'll be right there," Ms. Elgan said.

When they'd shut the door, Ashley turned to Ms. Elgan. "It was awful, wasn't it?"

"It needs some work," Ms. Elgan admitted tactfully. "It seemed a bit . . . forced. Insincere, perhaps."

"But I *was* sincere," Ashley insisted passionately. "I love the ranch with all my heart."

"Why?"

"Because it's the best place in the world. It's my home. There's a really good feeling about the ranch. You can see it in the horses. You can just tell they're happy there. And the people who come—they always leave smiling."

"It sounds lovely," Ms. Elgan said.

"It is. My friend Christina thinks the Pine Manor Woods around the ranch are sort of mysterious, that they contain a mystical force. All I know for sure is that when you're in those woods, you *do* feel different, like you've entered some other, really old, part of the world. Our trails go through those woods. I don't know. Maybe that's why people leave feeling so good."

"You make it sound truly special," said Ms. Elgan. "I'd like to visit your ranch myself some time."

"You should," Ashley assured her.

"Come on," said Ms. Elgan. "Let's go have some pizza."

They left the sound room and went back to the studio. They joined Christina and Ashley, who were already eating pizza and drinking soda.

"Where's Leonard?" asked Ms. Elgan as she took a slice of pizza from the open box set out on a folding chair.

"He said that if he worked fast, he might be able to show us a tape of the commercial today," Christina explained.

Just as they finished the last of the pie, Leonard returned. "If you want to come into the projection room, I can show you the commercial," he said.

"Let's see," said Ms. Elgan.

The girls followed her out of the room to another room several doors down. Inside it was dark except for the light coming from the projector. They found folding chairs to sit on, and Leonard began playing the commercial.

Ashley cringed at the sight of herself. She looked like a jolly marionette someone from above was working with invisible strings. She hated the sound of her voice. It was high and phony. And the words she spoke during the pictures *were* boring. Her commercial wouldn't convince anyone to come to the ranch.

There, in the dark, Ashley hung her head in embarrassment and despair. She'd just thrown a thousand dollars out the window!

14

The next day when Ashley got home from school she felt heavy, tired, and depressed. Ms. Elgan had assured her that she'd work on trying to fix the commercial up a bit, but Ashley didn't feel very hopeful. How much could she do with a commercial that bad? Ms. Elgan had also refused to take any money from Ashley—not until Ashley was satisfied with the results, she claimed.

At lunchtime, Trevor had walked right past her again without even looking at her. It had made her feel hurt all over again—and angry. Somehow, even though she knew in her head that he was a major jerk—and not worth her at all—it still hurt to be rejected. She wanted to smack him, to yell at him, to tell him that she didn't like him anymore, either.

During last period, she'd gotten back an English quiz. Her grade was a D, with a handwritten note from her teacher saying, *This is very disappointing. Please return with a parent's signature.* English was usually her best subject, too! But she just couldn't concentrate these days.

As she yanked open the freezer door, hoping to cheer herself up with some ice-cream, she noticed a note in her mother's handwriting tacked onto the refrigerator with a magnet. "Dad and I have gone to see Mr. Fisher in town," it read. "I will be back at around seven to take you guys to supper. Love, Mom."

Ashley stared at the note. It said *I* will be back, not *we*. Where would her father be? Why wasn't he coming back?

"They're signing the separation papers today, I think," said Jeremy.

Ashley looked up sharply. She hadn't even heard him come into the kitchen. "Separation?"

Jeremy nodded as he plopped down into a chair. "First they get separated, then they get divorced. That's how it works."

"Today?"

"I guess."

"Is Dad coming back to the ranch with Mom?"

"That note makes it sound like he's not."

"I know."

Feeling sick, Ashley took a chair beside Jeremy. "How could this be happening, Jeremy? I mean, do you understand it?"

Jeremy put his hand on her shoulder. He'd always been gentler and easier to talk to than Jason. "Not really. I know they've been fighting a lot."

"Is it just because of money, or are other things wrong between them?" Ashley asked.

"Who knows?" said Jeremy morosely. "I can't figure adults."

Ashley knew what he meant.

Jeremy went to the phone and began to punch in some numbers. "I'm going to see if anyone's around who might want to go into town and hang out. Do you want to come?"

"No, but thanks," she replied. It was nice of him to include her, since they didn't usually do things together.

Ashley got up and walked into the living room. The house suddenly felt like a lonely place, and unbearably quiet. She needed to get out of there.

Letting the door slam behind her, Ashley stepped onto the porch. Champ scrambled to his feet. She scratched his head absently and then began walking toward the stable.

She'd planned to visit Junior, but Champ decided to walk alongside her. A couple of the horses were skittish around him, so Ashley decided to keep walking past the stable into the woods.

The moment she stepped into the woods she knew she'd made the right decision. There was something soothing about the woods, something she needed, though she wasn't sure what it was, exactly.

After about fifteen minutes she realized she was headed for the Angels Crossing Bridge. Champ scrambled in and out of the stream that led to the bridge, enjoying the warm spring day.

When she got to the point where the stream disappeared at the base of the hill, she began to climb. Champ rushed up the hill ahead. At the top, she stood and looked down. There was the Angels Crossing Bridge.

Suddenly, unexpectedly, tears sprang to her eyes.

The bridge was empty. There were no angels. No deer. She would even have welcomed the sight of Ned and Norma. Angels or not, they'd always struck her as warm and understanding. But there was no one there— no one anywhere in the world who could help Ashley.

Never before had she experienced such terrible, empty, wrenching loneliness. It made her head spin, and she dropped to her knees. As the tears spilled from her eyes, she covered her face with her hands and sobbed.

Champ sat beside her and whined, a high, hollow song she'd never heard from him before. Blindly, she reached out and stroked him comfortingly, but he kept up his plaintive cry.

After her tears subsided, Ashley wiped her face. Champ licked her salty cheeks, forcing a sad smile onto her face.

She stood and began walking toward the bridge, not exactly sure why she was going there. Her footsteps on the bridge made the boards groan, and the noise blended with the scuffling of Champ's nails on the rough wood.

When she reached the middle of the bridge, Ashley looked down at the tumbling water of the creek below. She let its wild but steady motion lull her hypnotically. The steady burble and drubbing of the water began to sound like a sweet, soothing song inside her head.

After awhile, she felt very far away from everything. It was a good feeling, a relief. Ashley felt strangely peaceful, in a way she'd never felt before.

"Please," she heard herself whisper in a voice she hardly recognized as her own. "Please, somebody help me. I need help."

The sound of her own voice brought her back to reality. Looking to her side, she saw that Champ was watching the creek, too, his front paws up on the railing of the bridge.

She walked to the far end of the covered bridge and noticed a large cluster of tall purple wildflowers growing to the right of the bridge, extending all the way down to the creek. They looked a bit like wild heather, but Ashley had only seen heather bloom in August. Besides, the underside of the bloom was a strange, vivid pink. She'd never seen anything quite like this before.

Ashley snapped off a stalk and examined it more closely. The stems were rough, but the flower was smooth.

Alice knew a lot about plants and flowers. She might know what it was.

Ashley began gathering a bouquet of the strange flowers to bring back. The more she picked, the prettier they looked, all bunched together in her hands.

When she had as much as she could hold, she returned to the bridge. Champ was still gazing at the water, but he hurried to her side as she approached. Together, they left the bridge and went back up the hill.

As they walked back through the woods together, Ashley thought about the things that would happen next. Her mother would return and take them to Jimmy's Diner or Pizza King or someplace. Then she'd tell them that their dad had gone to live in a hotel for now, or maybe he was going to stay with his mother over in Miller's

Creek—but he wasn't coming home. Next she might ask them who they wanted to live with, or tell them they would be with her alone until the ranch was sold and . . .

Ashley couldn't think about it anymore. It was too painful. She just couldn't think about it.

As they walked out of the woods behind the stable, Champ spied a chipmunk and took off after it. Ashley took the opportunity to slip into the stable.

She found Junior still resting in his stall, with May keeping watch from the stall beside him. Ashley set her bouquet down in the hay and stroked Junior's neck. She remembered her parents' conversation about selling May if Junior died. She realized they'd given up hope—in Junior, in the ranch, and in themselves.

That was the worst part, Ashley decided. How could anything continue when there was no hope? How could Junior even get better if no one believed he would?

"*I* believe you can get better," she told the colt. She wasn't sure she *did* believe it, but saying the words made her feel better.

Outside, she heard Champ barking. She got up and went to see why he was making so much noise. He was barking at something she couldn't see inside the woods, probably a chipmunk or a squirrel. "Come on, boy," she shouted, clapping her hands for him to come.

Reluctantly, he left whatever he was barking at and followed her back up onto the porch. She scratched his head once more before he settled down to rest.

In the empty house she threw herself down into an easy chair in front of the TV and snapped on the set with the remote control. The local station came on.

Ashley was about to click to another station when she noticed the principal of her school, Mr. Marshall, on a panel talking about education in the county. Interested to see him on TV, she kept watching. But before he could say anything, the show went to a commercial break.

The first commercial was for a car dealership in Miller's Creek. Ashley watched it, impatient to get back to Mr. Marshall's program.

Suddenly, Ashley sat forward sharply in her chair. A familiar photo had come onto the TV screen. It was the Pine Manor Ranch!

Next, Ashley heard her own voice coming from the TV set. It was the strangest sensation.

But the commercial wasn't the commercial she'd seen —or even written.

As Katie's pictures flashed by, Ashley heard the words she'd spoken to Ms. Elgan in the sound room. "There's a really good feeling about the ranch," she heard herself say. "You can see it in the horses. You can just tell they're happy there. And the people who come—they always leave smiling . . . My friend Christina thinks the Pine Manor Woods around the ranch are sort of mysterious, that they contain a mystical force. All I know for sure is that when you're in those woods, you *do* feel different, like you've entered some other, really old, part of the world. Our trails go through those woods. . . . Maybe that's why people leave feeling so good."

Ashley's words finished just as the final photo flashed on the screen. It was the picture Katie had taken on the trail in the woods, the picture of the old bunkhouse taken through the trees.

"Wow!" Ashley murmured. *That* commercial was really good.

Ms. Elgan had come through for her, after all! But she hadn't even realized she was recording her words. This commercial was a total surprise.

Suddenly, Ashley remembered that she hadn't even paid Ms. Elgan yet. She'd assumed Ms. Elgan would expect the money when the commercial was finished. But Ashley hadn't known it would be finished and on TV so soon!

She ran to her room and took the ten hundred-dollar bills from her top drawer. Then she hurried to her mother's office, wrapped the money in a sheet of paper, and stuck it into an envelope. She addressed it to Ms. Eglan at the production studio and placed it in the basket of outgoing mail on her mother's desk.

Ashley didn't mind parting with the money. It hadn't been wasted, after all. This commercial was wonderful, better than she could have ever imagined.

She was flooded with a wave of hopefulness. The commercial really captured the beauty of the ranch. It would surely convince people to come.

And if the ranch was saved, maybe her parents' marriage would be saved along with it.

Ashley's smile suddenly melted into a thoughtful frown. What if things didn't happen fast enough? What if her parents got divorced and sold the ranch before the new customers began pouring in? She couldn't let that happen.

"I know!" said Ashley, the smile returning to her face as an idea occurred to her.

"All right!" Ashley cheered, punching the air. Wait until Mom and Dad saw this. They'd be so pleased and proud of her.

She jumped to her feet, filled with enthusiasm.

She'd call Mr. Fisher's office and tell them to come straight home. Together! Then she'd make a nice dinner—a romantic dinner, with candles on the table and flowers. She'd tell them about the commercial. If she left the TV on tuned to the local cable station, maybe it would even run again tonight, and she could show them.

Ashley went to the kitchen and pulled open several drawers. They had to have candles around somewhere. She found two blue ones and set them on the counter.

Now she needed flowers. She glanced around looking for the strange wildflowers she'd found. What luck she'd brought a whole bouquet home.

She didn't see the flowers. "The stable!" she exclaimed aloud, remembering she'd left them there.

Hurrying out the door, she ran to the stable to get the flowers.

"Oh, no!" she cried when she reached Junior's stall. She got there just in time to see Junior eating the last of the bouquet she'd left by his side. "Oh, well," she laughed softly. "I hope you liked them, hon."

She went back to the house and decided the next thing she should do was call her parents, but she only reached an answering machine. "This is Ashley Kingsley," she spoke after the tone. "Please tell Mr. and Mrs. Kingsley to come back home right away. It's very important."

They were supposed to be at his office. Why wasn't anyone answering the phone? she wondered.

15

Ashley spent the next hour making a salad, baking potatoes, and marinating some steaks she found in the refrigerator. She set a table for two in the kitchen, using the good dishes. In the middle of the table, she set out the two crystal candlesticks she'd found with the tall blue candles.

She didn't want to start cooking the steaks until she knew they were home. Where could they be? Had they even gotten her message?

The phone rang and Ashley snapped it up. "Mom?" she asked hopefully.

"No, it's me, Jason," came her brother's voice. "I guess Mom's not home yet. Tell her I ran into Jeremy in town with some guys, and we're grabbing a pizza. So we won't be home for her little 'Guess what kids, Dad's not coming home' announcement."

"That's not going to happen," Ashley said firmly.

"Sorry, Ashley. But you know that's the deal."

"It's not going to turn out that way," Ashley told him.

"You'll see."

"Dream on," said Jason. "So tell her. Okay?"

"I'll tell her . . . them . . . that you guys ate already," Ashley agreed. "Bye."

"Bye."

Feeling anxious, she stepped out onto the porch. It wasn't six o'clock yet, but it was getting dark. She looked up at the rain clouds gathering overhead. She saw Alice out in the pasture on horseback leading grazing horses in toward the stable.

Inside the house, the phone in the den rang. Hoping it was her parents this time, Ashley raced in to pick it up.

"Is this the Pine Manor Ranch?" asked a man on the other end.

"Yes it is," she told the man.

"That voice!" he cried happily. "You're the young lady on the commercial, aren't you?"

Ashley smiled proudly. "Yes, that's me," she said cautiously.

"When I saw that commercial, it brought back so many memories," the man said fondly. "My grandfather used to take me to your ranch during the summers when I was a boy. Those were the best weeks of my entire childhood. When I saw that building shot through the woods like that, I just couldn't believe it."

"Oh, the bunkhouse," Ashley said. "Yes, that's been empty for years now."

"It has?" the man said, sounding disappointed. "Too bad. That's why I was calling. You see, I have a tour business now, and I wanted to talk to someone about booking week-long vacations at your ranch. It would give me an excuse to visit again."

What a great idea! thought Ashley. It was a perfect way to bring fresh business to the ranch! "Oh," she whispered, hardly daring to hope.

"Hey, that gives me an idea," the man said, half to himself. "I've been looking for a new business investment. Do you think the owners would be interested in opening up again, say, as a kind of dude ranch or inn?"

"The owners are my parents, and I don't know," she replied. "But it sounds like an awesome idea to me," she blurted.

"It does, doesn't it," he chuckled. "I'd like to talk to them as soon as possible. Are they there?"

"Not right now, but I expect them back soon."

"Too bad. I'm leaving tomorrow for a month-long tour of Italy. If they don't get back to me tonight, it will have to wait for a month."

"Oh, they'll get back to you," Ashley said quickly. "How late can they call?"

"Well, normally I don't take calls at home, but I'll make an exception. They can reach me until ten or eleven at this number." The man gave her his name, Mr. Thomas, and his phone number.

"All right, Mr. Thomas," said Ashley. "I'll make sure they call before then. Thanks a lot for calling!"

"Thank *you*. Your commercial brought back some wonderful memories. I know what you meant about those woods. I remember feeling they were special, too. Well, nice talking to you. So long."

Ashley tried calling Mr. Fisher's office but got the machine again. She hung up without leaving a message. What was going on?

Back into the living room, she saw that her commercial was on again. She stood and listened to it, feeling pleased. When the last picture of the bunkhouse came on, she paid special attention. What good luck that someone who had once loved staying at the ranch had seen that picture!

It wasn't entirely luck, though. With Katie's help, she'd made it happen.

And she had to *keep* making things happen!

It was only a twenty-minute bike ride into Pine Ridge. She could make it there before dark and then catch a ride home with her parents. They were probably in some conference room or someplace without a phone. She had to tell them about Mr. Thomas's offer before they did anything legally. They *both* had to get back to him tonight. If they did, they might save the ranch.

They might even reconsider getting divorced.

Ashley stuck the paper with the phone number into her jeans pocket and went to the front hall, where she pulled on her denim jacket. Outside, she looked up at the rain clouds as she got her bike, which leaned on the side of the house. It was cloudy, but it looked like the weather would hold.

She rode her bike down the dirt road and turned left at the opening in the split-rail fence. The roads leading into Pine Ridge were narrow and winding, but Ashley had been riding them all her life.

When she was about halfway to downtown Pine

Ridge, Ashley felt the first drop of rain graze her cheek. Looking up, she saw that rain clouds had engulfed the sky. It was much darker than it should have been at that hour. It started to rain gently.

Bending her whole body to the task, she pedaled harder. With luck, she'd make it to Mr. Fisher's office before the sky really opened.

The cars driving by had turned on their headlights against the early darkness. The glare as they zoomed toward her was hard on her eyes. Sometimes the wipers whipped the water sideways and into Ashley's face.

The rain came down a little more heavily with every passing minute. Ashley's hair was dripping. From time to time she had to slow down to wipe away water rolling into her eyes.

As puddles formed the splashes from passing cars grew worse. Her pants were soaked from the knees down and flapped wetly at her ankles.

But Ashley couldn't stop. She *had* to reach her parents in time. Besides, she was already more than halfway.

Pedaling with fierce determination, Ashley kept her eyes trained on the white line along the side of the road. It was especially important to stay steady when she came to the curve of the road that ran along the ravine. A mistake here could be a hundred-foot plunge.

The driving rain now made it hard to see. Ashley's hair whipped water in her eyes. More water dripped down the neck of her jacket, and her legs felt heavy and stiff in her wet jeans.

Then she was jolted by the long, piercing blare of a

car horn as the vehicle careened too fast around a bend in the road.

Ashley felt the cold water of a puddle slam into her as if someone were dousing her with a hose.

Suddenly the lights from an oncoming car blinded her and she swerved slightly. She heard a terrible crunch as a passing car bumper tugged at her back wheel. The next thing Ashley kew, she was flying off her bike, sailing into the darkness.

With a blast of searing pain, she landed on the ground and banged her way uncontrollably down into the dark, rain-soaked ravine.

16

Ashley opened her eyes slowly. A line of pain cut straight across her forehead. It made her wince and shiver. She bit down on her lip to get things in focus.

Struggling to boost herself up onto her elbows, she peered up the sides of the ravine and saw the glare of headlights as cars zoomed by, spraying water behind them. Rain drubbed relentlessly on the young leaves of the trees.

It was darker than she remembered it being.

As a car passed by above, she saw her bike illuminated by the headlights. It was several yards up the ravine, bent in half around a young tree.

She realized it didn't matter anymore how wet she got. It wasn't possible to get more saturated than she already was. She was drenched down to her underwear.

Struggling forward onto her knees, Ashley attempted to get to her feet. But as soon as she pushed up with her hands, a wave of nausea washed over her.

Her stomach lurched.

She could hardly breathe.

Ashley leaned forward and threw up. Then she collapsed back down onto the wet, slippery ground. Her skin was cold and clammy, and she shivered violently.

She wanted to lay on the wet ground and rest, but she couldn't. She knew her life depended on getting out of that ravine. If she stayed down there, who knew how long it would be before anyone found her? It was getting cooler, too, and might go below freezing tonight.

Reaching forward, she grabbed hold of a tree and pulled herself up again. With all her weight on the tree she groped along, one hand over the other, until she was nearly standing.

The line of pain across her forehead burned until she imagined someone was aiming a blowtorch at her, trying to cut off the top of her head. "Owww!" she screamed out, trying to block the pain with the sound of her own voice. "Owww!" she howled as her knees buckled beneath her. "Owww!"

She was sliding down the tree. Her knees banged on the root of the tree. With a jarring crash, her head hit the ground.

Then she felt herself pulled backward into a churning, black ocean of nothingness—a cold sea threatening to pull her under.

Part of Ashley wanted to give up, to go under into the black, fathomless sea. Another part struggled to stay above the ever-moving surface.

Ashley slowly became aware of a pinpoint of light in the jet blackness. It grew brighter and brighter.

Was it some sort of star? It must be coming closer very quickly.

As the light grew brighter, a familiar face formed within the center of it.

"Ms. Elgan?" Ashley murmured.

The blackness quickly withdrew as if sucked up by the brightness of the light surrounding Ms. Elgan. Now Ashley lay in a calm world of blue light. She felt as though she were floating on a cushion of air, all pain gone.

"Ms. Elgan?" she asked again. What was Ms. Elgan doing there?

The woman smiled warmly and extended her hand. Ashley reached up and took it, allowing Ms. Elgan to draw her effortlessly up into a sitting position.

"How are you feeling, dear?" Ms. Elgan asked.

"Horrible," Ashley replied. "But actually not so bad now. I don't understand what's going on." Ashley looked all around at the calm, boundariless blue. "What are you doing here? Where are we?"

"We're in the in-between place." Ms. Elgan answered as Ashley continued to look everywhere.

"In between what?"

"My world and yours."

What was she talking about? What was going on?

Ashley looked back sharply.

Ms. Elgan was gone.

Edwina was there.

"Wha—" Ashley gasped. She didn't understand this at all.

Edwina's unearthly violet blue eyes shone with an inner radiance that lit her beautiful face. "I thought you were in France," Ashley finally stammered.

Edwina smiled. "Another young woman went to France instead. It was the break she'd been waiting for."

"What do you mean?" Ashley questioned.

"It's not important now," Edwina said. "You see, I only tried modeling for your sake."

"*My* sake?"

"Yes. I could see how important appearances were to you. You want to look just right all the time. You're impressed by the way things look in magazines. I needed to know about appearances if I was to help you."

"What did you find out?"

"That there are layers of truth beneath the surface appearance of things. And that appearances can be controlled so that things can appear to be what they aren't. I learned that, in the end, if you only have the appearance of beauty or the appearance of love, you don't have very much at all."

Ashley thought about Trevor, how he only liked her when she appeared to be the perfectly put-together girlfriend he wanted.

"But what about my family?" she asked Edwina. "We looked like the perfect family, and we all really love each other. I mean, I thought my parents really loved each other."

"Your parents panicked when they thought they would no longer *look* like the perfect family to the outside world."

"Is that why they're getting divorced?"

"For the most part," Edwina said. "They've lost track

of a few other things, too. But right now, we can't discuss it anymore. I can't let you stay here, in between, for too much longer. It's not good for human bodies."

Edwina got to her feet. "Wait!" said Ashley. "Then, you were Ms. Elgan all along?"

Edwina nodded as she pulled Ashley to standing with a soft hand that was comfortingly warm. "I would never forget you, and certainly not for anything as unimportant as modeling."

Now that they were both standing, Ashley saw that Edwina was dressed in a flowing white-and-gold gown. Shimmering iridescent wings fanned out from behind her.

Keeping hold of Ashley's hand, Edwina pulled her along. Ashley felt light, floaty. She had the idea that energy was pouring into her hand from Edwina, reviving her, healing her aching body. "Where are we going?" she asked.

Edwina didn't seem to hear her. Her glowing face was filled with calm concentration, as if her eyes were set on a goal way far in the distance.

Ashley began to panic. Where was Edwina taking her? Was she dying? Was Edwina taking her somewhere beyond her own world?

"Edwina!" Ashley shouted.

Suddenly, Edwina was gone!

Ashley found herself stumbling forward through icy blackness. What was happening?

The next thing she knew, she heard the sound of blaring horns, and she was engulfed in a blinding light.

17

A woman's face, fuzzy at first, slowly took shape before Ashley's eyes. "Edwina?" she murmured.

"It's Mom, honey."

Ashley realized that it *was* her mother, and she was crying. "Hank, she's awake," Mrs. Kingsley said, brushing the tears from her eyes.

Ashley's father came up alongside her mother. He touched Ashley's forehead with his strong, rough hand. "How's my girl?"

She wasn't sure. "Nothing hurts," she observed as she wiggled her fingers and toes to see if they were all right. She saw that she was in a hospital room. Rain splashed hard against the window to her right.

Mrs. Kingsley's face twisted with emotion, and she covered her face as she sobbed. "I'm sorry," she said, moving to the window.

"What's wrong?" Ashley asked, feeling stronger every moment.

"She's just very relieved," her father told her. "We

were both so shocked when we saw you staggering toward us on the road. Why were you there? What happened, sweetheart?"

As her head cleared, Ashley told him how she had tried to contact them at the lawyer's office but no one answered.

"Mr. Fisher's secretary had to go home, so he turned on the answering machine and we went into a conference room where we wouldn't be interrupted by the ringing phone," Mr. Kingsley explained.

"That's why I was coming to get you myself," Ashley said. "But then it started to pour, and a car forced me off the road. I got thrown down into the ravine. I guess I was climbing out of the ravine when you spotted me."

Mr. Kingsley shut his eyes at this news. "If you hadn't gotten out of there, we might not have found you in time," he said quietly. When he opened his eyes again, they were misted with tears.

"Did you get . . . separated?" Ashley asked. She had to know. It couldn't all have been for nothing. Had she been too late?

Mr. Kingsley pressed his lips together and looked uneasy. "No," he answered after a moment. "We were about to sign the papers when Mr. Fisher got up to check his messages. He told us there was a very important message from you saying to come straight home. When we called and no one answered, we got into the car and raced straight for home."

"And that's when you saw me on the road?"

Her face still blotchy, but looking calmer, Mrs. Kingsley returned to Ashley's bedside. "We were on the opposite side of the road when we spotted you. Another car was coming straight for you. Your father hit the brakes and leaned on the horn at the same time. The other driver hit his brakes and slid right into us instead of hitting you."

"Was anyone hurt?" Ashley asked.

Mrs. Kingsley shook her head and stroked Ashley's hair. "Just the cars. But you collapsed just as the cars collided. It all happened so fast. We didn't know if you were hit until we got out of the car and saw you lying there in the rain. Oh, Ashley why did you try to ride into town? Couldn't you see it was going to rain?"

"I thought I could make it to town before the rain. I didn't want you to get separated and—" Ashley suddenly remembered Mr. Thomas and his offer. "What time is it?"

"Eight-thirty," Mrs. Kingsley said, puzzled.

Ashley saw her wet jeans and sneakers draped over a chair. "There's a number in my jeans pocket. You have to call that number before eleven. A man wants to make a deal with you that might save the ranch."

"Is that what you were coming to tell us?" asked Mrs. Kingsley, looking at Mr. Kingsley.

"Yeah."

"Look what we almost did, Hank," Mrs. Kingsley said. "Look what we almost lost." Again, she broke down in tears. "I'll be back," she said, covering her face as she rushed from the room.

Mr. Kingsley's eyes darted back and forth between Ashley and the door. "Are you feeling all right?" he asked.

"I'm fine, I think," Ashley replied.

"I'd like to go talk to your mother a minute."

"Go ahead."

As Mr. Kingsley left the room, Ashley turned her head toward the rain-soaked window. Slowly she began absorbing and sorting out everything that had happened.

Edwina had been there all along. She'd given Ashley the money she needed but hadn't told her how to spend it. She'd shown up at the mall in the form of Ms. Elgan just at the moment when Ashley was about to throw away a chunk of the money to impress a boy who only cared about whether or not she *looked* right.

Edwina had reshaped the commercial so that it expressed the heart of how Ashley felt about her home. It had worked so well that it touched Mr. Thomas and inspired him to call.

Ashley wondered if Leonard was really Ned, all along. Probably, she decided.

Finally, Edwina had saved her life by getting her out of the ravine at the exact moment her parents were driving by.

Edwina had never really left her side at all. She'd been there all along. How could Ashley not have known!

Mr. and Mrs. Kingsley came back into the room. "Ashley, we want you to know something," said Mrs. Kingsley, sitting on the side of the bed beside Ashley. "Your father and I have had our eyes opened tonight. If we had lost you, we would both have been devastated. We've let our money problems drive us apart and haven't really looked at all that we have—all that we would lose if we let our family fall apart."

Ashley drew a sharp, hopeful breath. "Do you mean you're not getting divorced?"

"We're going to give everything more time and try to look at things differently," said her mother. "We think if we do that, things might work out."

"Which means no divorce," Ashley pressed.

"Divorce was never our first choice," said Mr. Kingsley. "So we hope we won't come to that."

"Yes!" Ashley cheered, but she felt suddenly light-headed.

"Rest," said her mother. "You seem remarkably all right considering what you've been through, but the doctors still want to check you for concussion and several other things. You'll be here at least overnight. We'll stay with you."

Ashley nodded and closed her eyes. She was feeling worn out all of a sudden. "Don't forget to call Mr. Thomas," she reminded them.

Mr. Kingsley fished the number from Ashley's jeans and squinted at it. "The ink has run, but I think I can read it," he said. "Judy, do you want to come with me and see what this Mr. Thomas has to say?"

"All right," Mrs. Kingsley agreed. "Ashley, you close your eyes and rest. We'll be right back."

"I'll be okay," Ashley murmured as she felt herself drifting back to sleep. Her parents left the room, and Ashley dozed off.

When Ashley awoke again, the room was dark. The rain had stopped, and raindrops glistened on the window, reflecting the light from the streetlight outside.

Mr. Kingsley snored, sprawled out in the leather chair

in the corner of her room. Ashley assumed her mother was around somewhere nearby.

She was about to close her eyes again when she noticed a square white box on the table beside her bed.

Reaching for the box, Ashley saw something written on top in elegant handwriting—"To Ashley, from Ms. E."

When Ashley lifted the lid she saw something inside shining amidst its crumpled tissue-paper cushioning. Gently lifting it out, she realized what it was—a glass figurine of an angel perched lightly on an amethyst crystal. The glass angel held up a prism ball that sparkled in the raindrop-scattered light of the street-light.

There wasn't any figurine in the collection Ashley had sold that compared to this one in its delicate beauty. Ashley held the glass angel to her heart as she leaned back against her pillow.

She heard footsteps padding into her room. "Everything all right, sweetie?" asked her mother, appearing at the end of her bed.

"Everything's okay."

"What's that?"

"A gift from a friend. Did anyone come to visit?"

"No, the nurse must have brought it in. How would your friend know you're here?"

"She's an amazing woman," Ashley said sleepily as she set the glass angel down on the end table. "It's unbelievable, the things she knows."

Mrs. Kingsley adjusted the blankets and Ashley felt herself drifting back to sleep. Soon she was in a deep, dreamless sleep.

She awoke again at dawn. The first morning light sparkled on the raindrops of the still-wet window. Ashley sat forward in awe. The walls of her room were awash in patterns of wavy rainbow color.

Blinking hard, she wondered what was going on.

Then she realized. The light was coming from the prism ball held by the glass angel on her table.

18

A week later, Dr. Jeffers walked out of the stable and smiled. "It's like a miracle," she said. "He's fit as a fiddle. It's like nothing was ever the matter with him. Junior will be just fine."

Ashley hugged her mother. "I knew he'd pull through! I knew it!"

Mrs. Kingsley laughed. "Then you were the only one who thought so."

"I don't understand it, either," Dr. Jeffers admitted. "Did you do anything out of the ordinary with him? Did you give him anything special to eat?"

"No," said Mrs. Kingsley thoughtfully.

"The flowers!" Ashley cried, suddenly remembering how Junior had eaten her bouquet. "I found these flowers in the woods, and Junior ate them by mistake."

"Really?" said Dr. Jeffers. "What did they look like?"

"Sort of like heather, but taller. And the blossoms were bright pink underneath."

"Heather in May?" asked Mrs. Kingsley.

"It seemed strange to me, too," Ashley agreed.

"Do you have any of these flowers left?" asked Dr. Jeffers.

"I could get you some," Ashley volunteered. "But it might take me a while to get to the spot and back."

"I don't want you to have to take a long walk right now," said Dr. Jeffers.

"I don't mind," said Ashley.

"Come have some lunch while you wait," Mrs. Kingsley offered Dr. Jeffers.

"That sounds wonderful. All right, Ashley, if you really don't mind getting the flowers, I'd love to see them."

As her mother and Dr. Jeffers headed for the house, Ashley headed toward the stable. She pushed open the door and saw Junior standing in his stall. The sheen was back on his palomino coat. His eyes were once again full of life. He whinnied at her just as he'd always done before he'd gotten sick. "I'll come back and see you later," she said to him happily. "I have to do something now." She blew him a kiss as she shut the stable door.

Ashley took off, running, around to the back of the stable and into the woods. It had taken her several days after she got out of the hospital to feel like her old self. She'd suffered a concussion and caught a cold, but for the last two days she'd felt more full of energy than ever before.

In the woods Ashley moved unwaveringly toward the stream. She was starting to feel confident in her ability to find the bridge.

At the stream, she slowed down, catching her breath as she followed its trail to the hill. Once again, she lost track of time as she went deeper and deeper into the thick, fragrant woods. At the top of the hill, she spied the bridge and broke into a run, kicking up pine needles as she thundered downhill.

She crossed the bridge, keeping a sharp eye for Ned, Edwina, or Norma. But all was quiet.

Ashley stopped short at the far end of the bridge.

There was not a single stalk of the strange, heather-like flowers anywhere. She walked down, closer to the creek. Nothing.

Could it be? she wondered. Could the exotic flowers that healed Junior have been another angel gift?

As Ashley stepped onto the front porch, she saw two large cardboard cartons sitting by the door. Her name was written across the top of each box in big, looping handwriting.

She knelt and carefully peeled back the brown tape sealing the first carton. "My dolls!" she gasped, lifting a flaxen-haired doll in an old-fashioned Dutch-girl outfit.

Opening the second box, she saw that it was padded with crumpled newspaper. Ashley unwrapped one wadded ball of paper. Her glass dragon figurine lay nestled inside. She unwrapped another. It was her glass dolphin. All her figurines were there!

The corner of a small white envelope appeared, wedged between two balls of paper. Opening it, she found a note. "We didn't need these anymore. Thought you might like them back."

Ashley cradled the small, shimmering dragon in her hand. She was so glad to have it back. Each delicate figurine reminded her of the person who'd given it to her or the special occasion she'd received it. She felt the same way about the dolls.

She noticed that her clothing hadn't been returned. Somehow that made sense to her. Ms. Elgan—or rather, Edwina—must have known that the clothing didn't mean as much to her as the dolls and the glass figures. Maybe back when she'd sold them Ashley had thought the clothes were important, but now, after everything that had happened, she knew they weren't.

People were important, her friends, her family. Her love of the ranch, even the horses, like Junior—those things mattered. Clothing just wasn't in the same category. Sure, it was fun to look good, but nice clothing just made a nice appearance. Appearances no longer seemed as important as they once had.

Jeremy came up the steps, startling Ashley. "What's that?" he asked as he glanced at the boxes.

"The stuff I sold at the tag sale. The person who bought it just returned some of it to me."

"Too bad," said Jeremy. "I guess he wants his money back.

"No," Ashley told him. "*She* doesn't."

"Wow!" That's nice of her," Jeremy said, looking surprised. "Weird, though. Why would anyone do that?"

Ashley shrugged. There was no way to explain it that would make sense to Jeremy. "Did you see the person who delivered these?" she asked, wondering if Edwina had been there.

Jeremy shook his head. "Nope. And I was out front helping Dad with the fence. No one drove in except Dr. Jeffers."

Ashley wondered how the boxes had gotten there. Jeremy stared at them as if he were wondering, too. "Oh, well," he said dismissively. "They're here."

"Yes, they are," Ashley agreed.

As Jeremy went into the house, Dr. Jeffers stepped out the front door. "Oh, there you are, dear. Did you find the flowers?" she asked.

"They weren't there," Ashley said. "I'm sure I looked in the right spot, but there wasn't a single one left."

"How strange," said Dr. Jeffers. "Too bad. Well, I'll look in my natural cures book and see if I can find anything that fits that description."

Ashley wondered if she would.

"Actually," Dr. Jeffers said suddenly, "the book's in my Jeep. Let's look it up now. Maybe you'll recognize it in one of the pictures."

Ashley followed her to the red Jeep parked by the stable. Dr. Jeffers opened the back and pulled out a canvas bag of books. "I always travel with these," she said with a smile. "I never know what information I'll need right on the spot."

She took a thick, leather-bound book from the bag. Leaning against the back of the Jeep she began thumbing through. "Medicinal flowers," she muttered absently as she searched. She looked up at Ashley. "You said it seemed to be in the heather family, didn't you?"

Ashley nodded. "But with pink bottoms to the flower."

Dr. Jeffers paged through the book for several more minutes, then held a page out to Ashley. "Is this it?"

"Yes!" Ashley cried as she looked at the delicate and precisely drawn picture of the flower. "Angelbloom," she said, reading the title above the picture. "That's it exactly!"

Ashley's mind raced. *Angel*bloom! Angelbloom! It had to have come from Edwina. That name couldn't possibly be a coincidence!

Dr. Jeffers took back the book and scanned it. Her brows knit thoughtfully as she read. "Well what do you know," she murmured. "It says angelbloom has powerful antibiotic properties and is believed to cure all sorts of infections."

"That explains it, then," Ashley said excitedly.

"Not quite," Dr. Jeffers replied, looking at Ashley with puzzled eyes. "The book also says that angelbloom is found only in Tibet, in the mountains. How did it get here?"

"I don't know," Ashley said. But maybe she did. "It's almost as if an angel planted it there," she said daringly.

Dr. Jeffers smiled good-naturedly. "That's an interesting idea," she said. "A lovely idea. But, really, seriously, it *is* extremely odd. Perhaps someone brought seeds into the country and they were somehow scattered and took root there." She got in her Jeep and started the engine. "Tell your mother I'll call in two days to see how Junior is doing."

"I'll tell her," Ashley called, waving as Dr. Jeffers pulled away from the stable. Somehow she was sure Junior would be perfectly fine.

Just then, Alice drove up in her brown pickup and parked nearby. Katie and Christina hopped out and hurried over to Ashley, who could see they were very, very excited.

Ashley was excited, too. She couldn't wait to tell them about the angelbloom. But she knew they must be excited about the meeting they'd just come from, with Sally Overton and the rest of the school paper's staff. "How did it go?" she asked before telling *her* news about the flowers.

"*What* go?" Christina asked.

"Your meeting, of course."

"Oh, that went fine," Katie said, "Sally loved Christina's column, so did everyone. And they liked my article about the tag sale. But come with us to the stable a minute. We *have* to show you something."

Just then, Ashley spotted her father and a tall man walking out of the bunkhouse. The man was Mr. Thomas. This was her chance to introduce her friends to him. It was important that they met him—or rather that *he* met *them*.

Ashley looked at her friends, then back toward the bunkhouse. "Can it wait just a few minutes?" she asked. "Dad is over with Mr. Thomas right now, going over more plans. I want to introduce you guys to him now, because he's going away for a month. He was supposed to leave last week, but he postponed his trip so Dad could start on the renovations while he was away. Maybe we can all get jobs when the bunkhouse opens up to tourists this summer."

"They're definitely going to open the place?" Katie asked.

"Yeah—and wouldn't it be cool if the three of us worked there together? Dad and Mom would probably hire you even without your meeting Mr. Thomas, but it would be better if you did. We could really earn a lot of money."

"I thought you were looking at material things differently these days," Christina reminded her with a smile.

Ashley grinned a bit sheepishly. "I am. But I still *like* clothes. I just don't think they're so important anymore."

"Okay," Christina considered. "I guess it's like, I *like* pecan pie, but I don't think it's a matter of life or death whether or not I get any."

"Exactly," Ashley agreed.

"We'll go see Mr. Thomas in a second," Katie said. "But you *have* to see what I brought to show you."

"Really, you do," Christina agreed.

"All right," Ashley gave in. "What is it?"

Katie grabbed hold of Ashley's wrist and pulled her over toward the stable. They kept going until they were behind it. "What?" Ashley laughed, catching their excitement.

Reaching into the inside pocket of her denim jacket, Katie pulled out a packet of photos. "I picked these up from the drugstore on the way to school," she explained. "They're my tag-sale pictures, and I wanted to hand them in along with my article."

"Wait until you see this," Christina said.

Katie pulled one photo from the pack and handed it to Ashley.

"Oh, my—" Ashley gasped when she saw the picture.

It was the photo Katie had taken the day of the tag sale, the one with Ashley, Christina, Ms. Elgan, and Leonard.

Only instead of a frizzy-haired older woman and her slightly nerdy assistant, the girls stood beside two majestic angels with gleaming wings and a heavenly light pouring from them—Edwina and Ned.

Christina looked at Ashley, her eyes bright with excitement. "I believed you when you told us Ms. Elgan was really Edwina, and Leonard was Ned," she said. "But now *everyone* will have to believe it. This is proof!"

Ashley looked at her two friends. What Christina said was true. They now had proof positive of the existence of angels.

"And listen to this," she said. She told them all about the angelblooms.

"Awesome," Christina said, wide-eyed.

"It can't be a coincidence," Katie agreed slowly.

"Edwina must have planted it there just for Junior," said Christina enthusiastically. "And I bet the angelbloom grew well there by the bridge because it's a powerspot, like they have in Tibet."

Katie scowled. "How do *you* know there are powerspots in Tibet?" she demanded skeptically.

"Oh, there have to be," Christina said confidently. "Tibet is a very mystical place. Like here. Once people know for sure there are powerspots and angels in the woods, they'll come flooding in!"

Suddenly, Ashley frowned. "I'm not sure I want the whole world to know," she said. "What if people from all over the place started tromping through the woods? It might spoil everything. Besides, we can't prove there are powerspots in the woods. The flowers are gone." She paused. "We *do* have the photo, though."

"Not anymore, we don't," Katie said suddenly in a dry, matter-of-fact tone. "Look."

Ashley glanced down at the photo. *"What?"*

The photo had changed. The angels were gone. "How did that happen?" Ashley cried.

All the photo showed was the three girls, their arms around one another, smiling together.

"Wait a minute," Katie said, taking the photo from Ashley. "How did I get into the picture? I *took* the picture."

"You're right," Christina said, looking at the photo.

The girls looked at one another in stunned bewilderment. After a moment Ashley smiled. "Maybe this picture is meant to remind us that miracles happen every day."

"You think?" Katie asked, studying the picture.

"Definitely," Ashley and Christina answered together.

They stood looking at one another a moment more. "Want to go meet Mr. Thomas now?" Ashley asked.

"Sure," Katie said.

As they walked along the woods toward the bunkhouse, Ashley glanced into the deep interior of the woods. It was a strangely wonderful feeling to know that whatever happened in the future, there was someone who cared about her, who knew what was going on.

She realized she'd never feel alone again. Now and forever, she'd trust that there was an angel at her shoulder.

FOREVER ANGELS

by Suzanne Weyn

Everyone needs a special angel

Katie's Angel
0-8167-3614-6 $3.25 U.S./$4.50 Can.

Ashley's Lost Angel
0-8167-3613-8 $3.25 U.S./$4.50 Can.

Christina's Dancing Angel
0-8167-3688-X $3.25 U.S./$4.50 Can.

The Baby Angel
0-8167-3824-6 $3.25 U.S./$4.50 Can.

Available wherever you buy books.

Rainbow Bridge®

FOREVER ANGELS
KATIE'S ANGEL

by Suzanne Weyn

Katie thought she was all alone in the world . . .

When her parents died, Katie's world turned upside down. Forced to move in with uncaring relatives, she's never felt more alone. Katie can't stop missing her parents, and it seems she's always getting into trouble for one reason or another. Finally she can't take it any longer and decides to run away. And that's when Katie discovers that she's not as alone as she thinks she is. There's someone special looking out for her—someone she never would have guessed—who can help Katie find the happiness she's been missing.

0-8167-3614-6
$3.25 U.S. / $4.50 Can.

Available wherever you buy books.

FOREVER ANGELS
CHRISTINA'S DANCING ANGEL

by Suzanne Weyn

All she wants to do is dance . . . like an angel

Christina dreams of dancing on air, but reality keeps bringing her down to earth. Her dance teacher thinks Christina should give it up, that Christina will never have the right build for dancing. Christina thinks where there's a will there's a way. If she can only make herself over, she's sure her wishes will come true. Her friends liked the old Christina just fine, and they're worried she's trying too hard to change. Christina is truly more special than anyone can guess, least of all Christina, but it will take a special being to make her see the light.

0-8167-3688-X
$3.25 U.S. / $4.50 Can.

Available wherever you buy books.

Rainbow Bridge®

FOREVER ANGELS

Win a Guardian Angel Pin!

500 winners!

Everyone needs a special angel. And now 500 lucky *Forever Angels* readers can have a special angel, too. A Guardian Angel *Pin* to wear with all your favorite outfits!

To enter the Guardian Angel Pin Giveaway just fill in the coupon below, or send us your name and address on a 3x5 card, and mail to: Forever Angels, Dept. B, Troll Associates, 100 Corporate Drive, Mahwah, NJ 07430.

- -

Please enter my name in the Guardian Angel Pin Giveaway.

Name _____

Address _____

City _____State _____Zip _____

Age_____Where did you buy this book?_____

Official Rules